Pirates, Shipwrecks,
and Historic Chronicles

Pirates, Shipwrecks
and Historic Chronicles

EDWARD ROWE SNOW

ILLUSTRATED

DODD, MEAD & COMPANY, NEW YORK

1 2 3 4 5 6 7 8 9 10

Library of Congress Cataloging in Publication Data

Snow, Edward Rowe.
Pirates, shipwrecks and historic chronicles.

Includes index.
1. New England—History, Local—Addresses, essays,
lectures. 2. Shipwrecks—New England—History—Ad-
dresses, essays, lectures. 3. Pirates—New England—
History—Addresses, essays, lectures. 4. Treasure-trove
—New England—History—Addresses, essays, lectures.
5. Tales—New England—Addresses, essays, lectures.
I. Title.
F4.5.S67   974   81–9798
ISBN 0–396–08027–8   AACR2

TO MY WIFE
ANNA-MYRLE SNOW
WITHOUT WHOM THIS
BOOK WOULD NEVER
HAVE BEEN ATTEMPTED
OR COMPLETED

Contents

Illustrations follow page 104

Part Five: Incredible Occurrences

Part Six: Shipwrecks

Part Seven: Supernatural Tales

Preface

As I put the finishing touches on this, my ninety-seventh volume, I look out across the 7-1/4-mile-expanse of ocean that is used by ships of all sorts and realize how lucky it is that I am by the edge of the North River, where more than one thousand sailing vessels were launched. From this vantage point sparkling water, breaking waves and a delightful coast with touches of glistening sand and rocky beach create the perfect atmosphere for the completion of this volume, which combines tales of pirates, treasure, shipwrecks, lighthouses and ghosts.

Over the years I have received so many letters from young people that for this book I have chosen stories which will appeal particularly to this group as well as to readers of all ages.

Institutions that have been of great help to me include the following: Marshfield's Ventress Library, the Scituate Library, the Hingham Library, the Boston Public Library, the Boston Athenaeum, the American Antiquarian Society and the Bostonian Society. The United States Coast Guard, which I admire so much, has helped when needed.

Those individuals I shall acknowledge, in addition to those who claim anonymity, are Samuel J. Parsley, Robert Sullivan, Fred Hooper, Police Officer Magee, Mrs. Doris Prosser, Dr. Jules Friedman, Paul Cantor, Richard Nakashian, Chester Shea, Marguerite Miller of the Daggett House on Martha's

Vineyard, Councilor John W. Sears, Suzanne Gall, Dorothy Snow Bicknell, Leonard Bicknell, Laura Bicknell, Jessica Bicknell, Eunice Snow, Donald Snow, Alfred Schroeder, Melina Herron Oliver, William Pyne, Frederick G. S. Clow, Trevor Johnson, Jean Foley, Walter Spahr Ehrenfeld, James Douglass, Arthur Cunningham, Marie Hansen, Richard Carlisle, Susan Williams, Elva Ruiz, Joel O'Brien, Joseph Kolb, Charles Marks and Frederick Sanford. I am extremely grateful to my secretary, Helen Salkowski, and to John Herbert of Quincy for their assistance in preparing this book.

EDWARD ROWE SNOW
Marshfield, Massachusetts

PART ONE

Pirates

CHAPTER 1

Captain Phillips,
Whose Head Was Pickled

John Phillips, whose head was brought to Boston in a pickle barrel, worked in the carpenter trade while a young man in his native England. He later resolved upon a seafaring life, shipping on a voyage to Newfoundland. The vessel was captured and the crew taken prisoner by the pirate Anstis. Evidently Phillips was soon attracted to the life of a marine highwayman: he signed pirate articles and became carpenter aboard Anstis's ship.

Phillips's initiation into the brutal side of piracy occurred when Anstis, sailing off Martinique, captured the ship *Irwin*, commanded by Captain Ross. A woman passenger aboard the *Irwin* was seized by a pirate and assaulted. Colonel William Dolly of Monserat forcibly intervened, whereupon he was terribly abused and severely wounded for his efforts to protect the unfortunate woman.

A short time later the pirates decided to try for a pardon from the English government. The members of the buccaneer band sailed to the island of Tobago. There they drew up a round robin, signing their names in a circle so that no one signature headed the list. In this petition they appealed to the King for clemency, claiming to have been forced to a life of crime by the master pirate Bartholomew Roberts. They further claimed that they loathed and despised the mere thought of piracy, and their only reason for capturing vessels was to use them as a means of escape, and to obtain a pardon.

This unusual message was sent to England aboard a merchant vessel from Jamaica. Several of the braver pirates also shipped on the merchantman, including John Phillips. On reaching England he went at once to some friends who lived in Devonshire. He was soon rudely awakened from his dream of clemency when he heard that other pirates who had returned with him had been locked in the British jail. Hurrying to Topsham, he again shipped on a voyage for Newfoundland, this time under Captain Wadham.

When he arrived safely on the American side of the Atlantic, Phillips jumped ship and, as the season was getting underway, became a Newfoundland fish splitter. At heart, however, he was still a dyed-in-the-wool pirate. Becoming better acquainted with his fellow fish splitters every day, he evaluated the character of certain of the men. He chose an auspicious moment to ask if they would care to exchange a fish-splitter's apron for the Jolly Roger. The answer was to his taste, a credit to his discernment. Sixteen of the men were in hearty accord with the suggestion.

At anchor in the harbor of Saint Peters, Newfoundland, lay a comfortable schooner belonging to William Minot of Boston. The pirates-to-be planned to seize this vessel on the night of August 29, 1723. But when the appointed hour arrived, only four of the sixteen summoned courage enough to make their appearance. Phillips was tired of fish splitting and decided to attempt the venture despite reduced numbers. The five men appropriated and sailed the schooner from the harbor without trouble.

When safely away, the pirates began to draw up articles but almost had to abandon this procedure when it was found there was no Bible on board upon which to take an oath. Finally one of the resourceful pirates found a hatchet, which was used instead of the Bible, and the ceremony continued. The articles for Phillips's newly christened ship *Revenge* included:

THE ARTICLES ON BOARD THE *REVENGE*

1. Every Man shall obey Civil Command; the Captain shall have one full share and a half in all Prizes; the Master, Carpenter, Boatswain, and Gunner shall have one Share and quarter.

2. If any Man shall offer to run away, or keep any Secret from the Company, he shall be maroon'd with one Bottle of Powder, one Bottle of Water, one small Arm and Shot.

3. If any Man shall steal any Thing in the Company, or game to the Value of a Piece of Eight, he shall be maroon'd or shot.

4. If at any Time we should meet another Marooner that Man shall sign his Articles without the Consent of our Company, shall suffer such Punishment as the Captain and Company shall think fit.

5. That Man that shall strike another whilst these Articles are in force, shall receive Moses' Law (that is, 40 Stripes lacking one) on the bare Back.

6. That Man that shall snap his Arms, or smoak Tobacco in the Hold, without a Cap to his Pipe, or carry a Candle lighted without a Lanthorn, shall suffer the same Punishment as in the former Article.

7. That Man that shall not keep his Arms clean, fit for an Engagement, or neglect his Business, shall be cut off from his Share, and suffer such other Punishment as the Captain and the Company shall think fit.

8. If any Man shall lose a Joint in Time of an Engage-

ment, he shall have 400 Pieces of Eight, if a Limb, 800.

9. If at any Time we meet with a prudent Woman, that Man that offers to meddle with her, without her Consent, shall suffer present Death.

Phillips was made captain. John Nutt became navigator, James Sparks gunner, and Thomas Fern carpenter. William White, whose career ended later in Boston harbor, became the single crew member. It was not long before he had company, for the piratical cruise gathered ships and men. Some willingly joined the pirates; others had to be forced. Among the former was John Rose Archer, who had already served in illustrious company with Blackbeard, as bloodthirsty a villain as ever hoisted the Jolly Roger. Based on his background of buccaneering bravery, Archer was made the ship's quartermaster.

September 5, 1723, was a busy day for the pirates. They captured several fishing vessels off Newfoundland and forced three men into service: Isaac Larsen, an Indian; John Parsons; and John Filmore, the great-grandfather of President Millard Fillmore.

Later in the month Captain Furber and his schooner were taken. The Massachusetts Archives reveal that the next capture was a French vessel, from which the pirates removed thirteen pipes of wine, many supplies and a large cannon. Two of the crew, Peter Taffrey and John Baptis, were forced into service.

Early the next month an important capture was made. The buccaneers overtook the brigantine *Mary,* under Captain Moor, and removed her cargo worth five hundred pounds. A few days later another brigantine fell to the pirates. This time a William Taylor joyously accepted membership in the pirate crew. According to his words, he was being taken to Virginia to be sold when "they met with these honest men and I listed to go with them." Just how honest Taylor eventually found the pirates is a question.

Ship after ship was captured as the pirates continued their profitable undertaking in the West Indies. Eventually, however, their fortunes changed and provisions ran low. When the meat rations were practically exhausted, they ran afoul of a French sloop from Martinique, mounting twelve guns. Ordinarily they would have sailed clear of this formidable opponent, but hunger made them reckless. Hoisting the black flag, Phillips ran alongside and shouted that unless immediate surrender was made, no quarter would be given. The French crew unexpectedly gave in at once. The buccaneers plundered the sloop and took four of her men, then allowed her to sail away.

By this time the bottom of the *Revenge* needed cleaning. The ship was sailed to the island of Tobago, where she was run up at high tide and careened. Bad news awaited the pirates: their old buccaneering associates had all been taken to Antigua and hanged. As the *Revenge* was having the heavy sea growth removed from her sides and bottom, the masts of a man-of-war became visible on the leeward side of the island. In hot haste the *Revenge* was launched and sailed from the harbor at the flood of the tide, leaving four Frenchmen on the beach.

For the next few days in February 1724 the pirates followed a northerly course, sailing some distance to the south of Sandy Hook. They soon fell in with Captain Laws, master of a snow bound for Barbados. Thomas Fern, James Wood, William Taylor and William Phillips (not to be confused with Captain John Phillips) were sent aboard the square-rigged ship and ordered to keep company with the *Revenge*. The two vessels pursued a southern course until Latitude 21°, whereupon Fern, disgruntled because Archer had been made quartermaster, tried to run away with the snow. Captain Phillips was on the alert, however, and gave chase.

Drawing alongside, he ordered Fern aboard the *Revenge*. For a reply Fern fired his pistol at Captain Phillips, missing him. A short skirmish ensued; Wood was killed, William Phillips badly wounded in the leg, and Taylor and Fern forced to surrender.

Something had to be done at once for William Phillips, in agony from his wound. The decision was made to amputate. The ship's carpenter, because of his experience in sawing, was chosen to perform the operation. He went below and soon appeared on deck with the largest saw he could find in his chest. Taking the painfully injured leg under his arm, he fell to work. Finally the limb dropped off the injured man's body. To seal the wound, the carpenter heated his broadax white-hot and seared the leg as best he could. The operation proved a complete success. Shortly after the operation a fishing schooner was captured. The pirate captain suggested Phillips be put aboard, but the injured man demurred, fearing he would be hanged upon reaching the mainland. He chose to convalesce with the pirates, and he lived on to be tried later as a pirate, condemned and pardoned.

Within a short time the buccaneers seized a ship from London, from which they removed cannon and powder. An expert navigator, Henry Giles, was forced from this ship to the *Revenge* with his "Books and Instruments." Since he was a man of importance and education, sailing master Nutt placed him in charge of the journal.

Soon Fern again attempted escape. This time Captain John Phillips promptly shot and killed him. Another person who tried to get away a little later was also summarily put to death. The rest of the forced men decided to be more cautious, having plans afoot, however, for eventually taking over the *Revenge*.

Two ships from Virginia were now captured, one of them in charge of another Captain John Phillips. The second ship was commanded by Captain Robert Mortimer, a young married man on his first trip as a master. While pirate Phillips was aboard Mortimer's ship, he heard of a mutiny on his own vessel. Captain Mortimer quickly seized this opportune moment to start a fight of his own. Grabbing a handspike, he hit Phillips on the head. The blow either lacked force or Phillips's head was singularly hard. He staggered back, drew his sword and ran Mortimer through. At once two of the pirate's men cut Mortimer to pieces. Mortimer's own men, frightened at the bloodshed, stood by without offering a hand to help their captain.

Two men were forced from the other ship: seaman Charles Ivemay and carpenter Edward Cheeseman, needed to replace Fern. John Filmore, while rowing Cheeseman across to the *Revenge,* found the opportunity to discuss certain plans with the carpenter, schemes that called for the eventual seizure of the *Revenge.* Cheeseman gave his heart and soul to the idea, and from that moment the perfection of details which brought final escape was effected.

Resuming the cruise, the pirates captured eleven vessels in rapid succession. William Lancy, captain of a fishing schooner, was brought aboard the *Revenge* and while there saw nine vessels overhauled and captured. One of the captains gave the pirate a merry chase but was finally taken. Captain Phillips, enraged at this lack of consideration, ordered the unlucky commander, Dependence Ellery, aboard the *Revenge.* He was prodded around the deck and made to dance and jump until he collapsed in a dead faint.

Now begins the voyage that ended in the death of Phillips. On April 14, 1724, Captain Andrew Haraden sailed from Annisquam for a trip aboard the *Squirrel,* his new fishing boat whose deck was not quite finished. Leaving Ipswich Bay, the sloop fell in with another vessel, which was actually the pirate ship *Revenge.* Off the Isles of Shoals Captain Phillips sent a shot across the sloop's bow and ran up a black flag with a skeleton on it. When Haraden saw that the situation was hopeless, he rowed to the *Revenge* and surrendered. Phillips liked the lines of the *Squirrel* and ordered all stores transferred to the trim sloop. The other fishermen were allowed to go aboard the *Revenge* and sail for home, but Haraden was forcibly detained on his own vessel, which now became the pirate flagship. Before long Cheeseman approached Haraden with ideas of escape; Haraden was very interested.

Several of the forced men believed that the best time to capture the sloop was at night. But the presence of tall, husky John Nutt proved a stumbling block. The conspirators finally decided it would be too risky to try to take him without firearms. Cheeseman suggested a daylight attempt, when there would be less chance for confusion, and the conspirators agreed upon this plan. High noon on April 17, 1724, was chosen as the most appropriate time. The various tools of the carpenter could be placed around the unfinished deck, on which men were working. Then, at a given signal, the attack was to be made with the tools as weapons.

The moment arrived. Cheeseman brought out his brandy bottle, took a drink and passed it to John Nutt, offering as a toast that they should all drink to their next meeting. Then Cheeseman and Nutt took a turn about the deck. Passing a broadax lying on the planks, Filmore casually picked it up. Holding it carelessly in his hand, he watched Cheeseman as the latter asked Nutt what he thought of the weather. Before Nutt could answer, Haraden winked knowingly at the other forced man, whereupon Cheeseman thrust a hand between the astonished Nutt's legs, grabbing the sailing master by the collar with the other hand. Striding across the deck with the struggling pirate, he attempted to throw Nutt over the side. But Nutt grabbed frantically at Cheeseman's coat sleeve, crying, "Lord, have mercy upon me! What are you trying to do, carpenter?"

Cheeseman answered that it was obvious what was happening. "Master, you are a dead man," he cried. Striking Nutt heavily on the arm, Cheeseman watched the pirate fall to his death in the sea.

Meantime there was plenty of action elsewhere on the sloop. When Filmore saw the sailing master being thrown to his death, he split the boatswain's head clear down to his neck in one mighty blow. Captain Phillips rushed on deck just in time to receive a terrific blow on the head from a mallet wielded by Cheeseman. This broke the pirate's jaw, but Phillips leaped for his assailant. Haraden then sprang at the captain. Cheeseman, seeing Gunner Sparks trying to interfere, tripped him, causing him to fall into the way of the two Frenchmen, who hurled him into the sea.

Haraden now brought his trusty broadax down on the captain's head, killing him instantly. Cheeseman started toward the hold looking for John Rose Archer, the quartermaster. Encountering him in the runway, Cheeseman hit Archer two or three times with his mallet, but as he was about to finish him off, he heard someone shouting, "Stop!" It was Harry Giles, the young seaman, who said that some of the pirates should be taken alive as evidence. Recognizing the wisdom of this, Cheeseman bound Archer and three other pirates hand and foot with ropes.

Captain Haraden was again in command of his sloop. While the *Squirrel* was running for Annisquam, the sailors cut the head from the body of Captain John Phillips and affixed it to the mast of the sloop for a time.

Sailing up the bay, Captain Haraden ordered a gun fired to announce their happy homecoming. Unfortunately the gun went off prematurely, killing the French doctor on board. It is probable that the bodies of several of the pirates who had been killed in the struggle were taken ashore at Hangman's Island, in Annisquam harbor. Tradition, always a little at fault, has it that the men were hanged at the island. But they were already dead, so it seems likely that their bodies were strung up in chains to warn other pirates. There is no evidence on this point, however. The heads of Captain John Phillips and another pirate, Burrill by name, were brought to Boston in a pickle barrel to preserve them for evidence.

The *Boston News-Letter* estimated the pirates' victims as three shallops, fifteen fishing vessels, three schooners, three brigantines, four sloops, and five ships—thirty-three vessels that Phillips had captured in less than eight months.

Captain Andrew Haraden had now the not-too-easy task of proving his own innocence. He at once went to the "Harbor," as the present Gloucester was then called. There he made oath before Esquire Epes Sargent, swearing the details of his capture by the pirates and his eventual delivery. He then returned to the sloop to await investigation. Shortly afterward, on May 3, the four real pirates and the seven forced men were all locked up in the Boston jail.

The Court of Admiralty, with its customary pomp and ceremony, was held in Boston on May 12, 1724, to try the men accused of piracy. Lieutenant Governor William Dummer, erstwhile commander of the great fort at Castle Island, presided at the court in what is now the Old State House. Skipper Haraden, who does not seem to have been brought to trial, gave important testimony as to the character of John Filmore and Edward Cheeseman, who were tried first. When Haraden told of the events of April 17, in which Filmore and Cheeseman fought so effectively against the pirates, the court was visibly affected. Dummer ordered the room cleared, and the verdict of "not guilty" came as welcome news to the two accused men.

Later that day the court sat again. This time one-legged William Phillips, navigator Henry Giles, Indian Isaac Larsen, and other pirates were brought to the bar. When it was revealed that Larsen had held Captain Phillips's arm when Haraden struck him with the adz, the court seemed favorably inclined toward the Indian. Filmore said that he had never seen Larsen guilty of piracy except when "they now and then obliged him to take a shirt or a pair of stockings when almost naked." William Phillips, who had lost a leg, claimed to have been a forced man, but the evidence seemed to prove his guilt.

William White, the only one left of the original five who captured the sloop at Newfoundland, was then brought in. Filmore, who had been at Newfoundland when the sloop was stolen, testified against him. Filmore said that White admitted he had been drunk when he joined up. William Taylor had so often been in conference with Captain Phillips that he was adjudged guilty. John Rose Archer, whose record was very bad because of his previous service with Blackbeard, was found guilty along with William Phillips and William White. The two Frenchmen were pardoned when it was shown that they had assisted in defeating the pirates. Phillips and Taylor were also reprieved, so there were only two pirates left in government custody on the date of execution, June 2, 1724. All others had been pardoned, for one reason or another.

Cotton Mather preached his usual sermon to the condemned men on May 31, 1724. According to Mather, both pirates had requested the sermon. Afterward Mather conversed with the condemned men privately, and believed them truly repentant.

Before the hangman sprung the trap, both pirates gave substantial speeches of penitence. Said Archer:

> I greatly bewail my profanations of the Lord's Day, and my Disobedience to my Parents. And my Cursing and Swearing, and my blaspheming the Name of the glorious God. . . .
> But one Wickedness that has led me as much as any, to

all the rest, has been my brutish Drunkenness. By strong Drink I have been heated and hardened into the Crimes that are now more bitter than Death unto me.

I could wish that Masters of Vessels would not use their Men with so much Severity, as many of them do, which exposes us to great Temptations.

William White followed with his parting message. Probably Cotton Mather had helped him compose the details.

I am now, with Sorrow, reaping the Fruits of my Disobedience to my Parents, who used their Endeavours to have me instructed in my Bible, and my Catechism. . . .

But my Drunkenness has had a great Hand in bringing my Ruin upon me. I was drunk when I was enticed aboard the Pyrate.

The usual large gathering of Boston people then watched the two men climb the ladder to the scaffold. At one end of the gallows the black pirate flag had been hung, the skeleton on it dancing in the wind as the men climbed the last rungs. The local paper said that the flag gave the whole affair "the sight dismal." At the signal the two pirates were left hanging in the air. So died pirate John Rose Archer, age twenty-seven, and pirate William White, age twenty-two, between the rise and fall of the tide at the Charlestown Ferry in Boston. A few hours later their bodies were cut down, placed in an open boat and taken to Bird Island, whose low-lying flats were between Noddle's Island and Governor's Island.

Down at Bird Island, meanwhile, Marshall Edward Stanbridge busily superintended the erection of a gibbet. Measurements had been made of Archer's head and the local blacksmith had turned out a wide iron band that fit nicely. Other iron bands were made to go around Archer's chest, hips and ankles, with chains connecting the various bands to keep them from slipping. On the arrival of the bodies at the island, White was quickly buried. Archer, who had been with Blackbeard, was hung in chains as an example for all to see. The iron bands and the chains, together with the hire of an extra man to help secure the bands and chains, cost twelve pounds ten shillings.

So the body of Archer swung in the wind, its iron bands creaking rhythmically, a reminder of the awful fate awaiting pirates. Bostonians made excursions and trips out to Bird Island to see at close range the gruesome sight. One good citizen, Jeremiah Bumstead, a brazier by trade, took his wife and ten friends down the harbor six days after the execution to see the "piratte in Gibbits att Bird Island."

In later years Bird Island washed away completely. Today it is only a memory, like the pirate who hung there and the captain's pickled head.

CHAPTER 2

Marblehead's Crusoe

Every reader knows and marvels at the tale of Robinson Crusoe. Less known, yet perhaps more incredible, is the story of Philip Ashton of Marblehead, who in three years lived through more adventures on the seas than most men could experience in a lifetime.

The exploits of this young Marblehead sailor began while he was with the fishing fleet in waters off Cape Sable. At that time, 1722, it was customary for the entire fleet to stop fishing on Friday afternoon and sail into Port Roseway, near what is now Shelburne, Nova Scotia, to await the Sabbath and observe it there. As the shallop carrying Ashton entered Port Roseway on June 15, 1722, he noticed not only the usual number of fishing boats in the harbor but a brigantine, which he incorrectly assumed to be an inward-bound West Indiaman.

Shortly thereafter a boat from the brigantine came alongside Ashton's shallop. Suddenly the men in the boat jumped aboard the fishing vessel and pulled out cutlasses and pistols, soon overcoming the astonished fishermen. This maneuver was repeated until more than a dozen fishing vessels anchored in the harbor had been captured.

When the fishermen were brought aboard the brigantine, they found that it was commanded by none other than the infamous villain, Captain Edward Low.

Philip Ashton was soon sent for, and he went aft to meet the notorious pirate. Confronted by the man whose name alone was enough to strike terror in the hearts of all honest sailors, Ashton was asked to sign articles and go along on a voyage. In his own words, Philip Ashton tells us what then occurred:

> I told him, No; I could by no means consent to go with them, I should be glad if he would give me my Liberty, and put me on board any Vessel, or set me on shoar there. For indeed my dislike of their Company and Actions, my concern for my Parents, and my fears of being found in such Bad Company, made me dread the thoughts of being carried away by them; so that I had not the least Inclination to continue with them.

When Ashton refused to join up and sign articles with Captain Low, he was roughly handled and thrown down into the hold. While there he heard the various crews of the fishing fleet being brought over to the brigantine, one by one, and realized that there was little hope of assistance from the other vessels. The next day about thirty or forty of the fishermen who had refused to join up were placed on Mr. Orn's fishing schooner, which was turned into a floating prison for the dissenters.

At noon on Sunday Quartermaster John Russel boarded the schooner and took away six of the fishermen. They were Nicholas Merritt and Lawrence Fabens, both of whom later escaped; Joseph Libbie, who finally became a pirate and was hanged at Newport; Philip Ashton; and two other men whose names are not known. The fishermen were rowed over to the pirate chieftain's flagship, where they were lined up on the quarterdeck. All of them were under twenty-one years of age.

Captain Ned Low approached them, pistol in hand. "Are any of you married men?" asked Low. The question, unexpected as it was, struck the listeners dumb for the moment. The silence infuriated the pirate, and he cocked his pistol, shoving it against the head of poor Philip Ashton. "You dog," cried Low, "why don't you answer me? I shall shoot you through the head unless you tell me now if you are married or not."

Ashton, greatly frightened, stammered that he was not married, and the rest of the group answered similarly. Low then walked away. Ashton later found out that the pirate's concern was due to Low's wife having died, leaving a small child, who even then was living in Boston.

Later in the day Low again interviewed the six men and asked them to sign papers. All refused. Still later he had each man sent for singly, whereupon he repeated the question. Each fisherman again refused. Then Philip Ashton was taken below into the steerage, where the quartermaster tried to tempt him with stories of great riches and wealth. Other pirates gathered about him and tried to be friendly, to win his confidence. They asked him to "drink with them, not doubting but that this wile would sufficiently entangle me, and so they should prevail with me to do that in my Cups, which they perceived they could not bring me to do while I was Sober; but . . . I had no Inclination to drown my Sorrows with my Senses in their Inebriating Bowls, and so refused their Drink, as well as their Proposals."

After his final refusal Ashton was taken back up on deck, where Captain Low threatened him with death unless he changed his mind. Ashton said that whatever happened he could not join the pirate band. Eventually Low signed him on as a forced man, together with all his companions.

The following Tuesday the buccaneers chose a schooner belonging to Joseph Dolliber of Marblehead as the new flagship, and all the pirates went aboard her. With the exception of the six forced men and four others who had joined from the Isles of Shoals, the prisoners were sent over to the brigantine and allowed to proceed to Boston. This was discouraging to Philip Ashton, who made one final attempt to appeal for freedom. He and Nicholas Merrit went to Low, falling on their knees before the pirate captain and asking for release. Low scornfully refused, telling them if they attempted to escape they would be shot. The brigantine soon sailed off, and the forced sailors were alone with the highwaymen of the sea.

Just as Ashton had given up all thought of deliverance, an accident occurred that gave him hope. One of the pirates had left a dog on the beach when he came back to the ship, and the dog began to howl dismally. Low, hearing the disturbance, ordered that the dog be brought out. Two Marblehead boys volunteered to row in and get him, and nineteen-year-old Philip Ashton decided this was a good chance to escape. He rushed to the side of the ship and was about to jump into the boat, but Quartermaster Russel caught hold of his shoulder, saying that two men were sufficient to bring out one dog.

The pirates watched the boat land on shore and the Marblehead men walk inland away from it. They never returned, and the pirates lost their boat as well. The dog soon wandered off and was not seen again.

Quartermaster Russel believed that Ashton had tried to join the two, knowing that they planned to escape. But the truth was that while Ashton had planned to flee, he did not know the other two had the same objective. Nevertheless, the quartermaster was so infuriated that he attempted to kill Ashton then and there.

Russel seized Philip Ashton by the shoulder, clapped his great pistol against his skull and pulled the trigger. The gun misfired. Again and again the quartermaster snapped the pistol, but each time it failed to go off. Disgusted with his firearm, Quartermaster Russel went over to the side of the ship. Standing by the rail, he reset the pistol, pulled the trigger and fired the gun successfully into the ocean. The exasperated pirate now drew his cutlass and lunged for the boy. Terrified, Ashton ran down into the hold, where he cowered in the midst of other pirates, thus escaping Russel's further wrath.

It was a hard lot that lay ahead for the Marblehead lad, and he soon learned to hide in the hold most of the time. Once a week, however, he was brought up under examination and asked to sign articles, and every time he refused. Thrashed and beaten with sword and cane after each refusal, Ashton would escape to the hold as soon as he could to nurse his cuts and bruises for another week. Probably some of the kinder-hearted rogues took care of him in their crude way, so that he was able to get something to eat every day.

Week after week passed without hope, and despair made Ashton utterly miserable. In the book he later wrote, he speaks of Low's narrow escape from an encounter with a British man-of-war in the very harbor of Saint John's, Newfoundland, mentioning the seizure of seven or eight vessels the next day. Later a captured sloop manned by impressed pirates ran away from Low and was never seen again. Nicholas Merrit, one of Ashton's Marblehead friends, was aboard this vessel. The schooner and a captured pinkie were careened at the island of Bonavista, after which seven or eight forced men from the pinkie went ashore to hunt. They never returned to the ship. With so many escaping from Low, Ashton felt that his chance would eventually come. In this he was not mistaken.

A terrible storm caught the pirates shortly afterward, and for five days and nights Ashton feared that they would all go to the bottom. Even the most foul of the buccaneers was afraid during the fearful tempest, as Ashton recorded one of the bloodthirsty ruffian's exclaiming in his particular moment of spiritual anguish, "Oh! I wish I were at Home."

At last the storm subsided and the pirates headed for the

three islands called the Triangles, located in the West Indies about forty leagues from Surinam. Captain Low decided that another careening was necessary. In heaving down the pinkie, so many hands climbed into the shrouds that it threw her open ports under water. Low and the doctor, below in the cabin, almost drowned but managed to get out in time. The vessel went over on her beam ends in forty feet of water, throwing the men into the sea. As the vessel righted itself, the men climbed back into the shrouds. The entire hull remained far under water. It had been a narrow escape for the notorious Captain Low.

In the excitement two men drowned. Ashton, who was a poor swimmer, almost perished before he was rescued. The pinkie had carried most of the provisions and the drinking water, both of which were lost, so every sailor transferred to the schooner, which at once put out to sea.

Reaching the island of Grand Grenada, eighteen leagues westward of Tobago, they went ashore for water. The French on the island, suspecting them of being in the smuggling trade, sailed out to capture Low and his men. When Low saw them coming he ordered all the pirates to their stations, and the French sloop was quickly seized and made one of the pirate fleet. The buccaneers captured seven or eight vessels in short order, then took two sloops off Santa Cruz.

Low now desired a doctor's chest. He sent four Frenchmen ashore at Saint Thomas, demanding of the residents a chest of instruments and medicines or their town would be sacked and burned. The doctor's chest arrived within twenty-four hours, and the Frenchmen who had been prisoners were allowed to sail away in one of the captured sloops.

From Santa Cruz the pirates sailed to Curaçao, where they encountered an English man-of-war and a "Guinea-Man." Low escaped by sailing over some shallows on which the man-of-war ran aground. On this occasion Ashton was aboard the schooner, under command of Quartermaster Farrington Spriggs. The two pirate vessels separated in the chase, with Spriggs heading for the island of Utilla, near Roaton. Having lost Low completely, Spriggs decided to sail up through the Gulf of Mexico to New England, where he could increase his small company and reprovision his schooner.

There were eight forced men in Spriggs's entire crew of twenty-two who secretly plotted to capture the schooner. The scheme was to get the pirates drunk under the hatches as soon as the *Happy Delivery* approached the shores of New England. The forced men would then sail into the nearest harbor and throw themselves on the mercy of the government.

It was a good plan, but the men never had a chance to try it. Sailing from Utilla they fell in with a large sloop, which bore down on them, opening fire as it approached. Spriggs did not come about, running for possible escape instead. Then pirate colors were hoisted from the sloop. At this the regular pirates aboard Spriggs's vessel broke into cheers, for it was none other than Low's famous ensign that fluttered high above the sloop's decks. Soon the two old cronies were together again, and all was well except for the forced men, whose scheming came to an end. In the five weeks that Low and Spriggs had been separated, the forced men had hoped they had seen the last of the villain. But such was not the case. To make matters worse, one of the forced men eventually informed on the others. Spriggs was in favor of shooting them down, but Low laughed it off.

On returning to the schooner, Spriggs told Ashton he deserved to be hanged from the yardarm. Ashton informed the schooner's captain that his only desire was to be free of the pirate vessel, and he intended to harm no one. The incident was soon forgotten.

Low now steered a course for Roatan harbor, in the Bay of

Honduras. The pirate chieftain went ashore to indulge in drinking and carousing for a few days while his buccaneers were occupied careening and scraping the vessels. The schooner was loaded with logwood and sent out in charge of John Blaze, with four men aboard. When Low and Spriggs, together with many of the pirate leaders, went off to another island, Ashton's hopes were raised again. He would try to escape.

Saturday, March 9, 1723, was an eventful and thrilling day for Philip Ashton. Noticing the cooper with six men getting ready to row ashore from Spriggs's vessel, he impulsively asked to be taken with them, as he had not been on land since his capture almost nine months before. Since the island was desolate and uninhabited, the cooper finally gave in to the pitiful pleadings of the lad from Marblehead. Young Philip jumped into the longboat, dressed "with only an Ozenbrigs Frock and Trousers on, and a Mill'd Cap upon my Head, having neither Shirt, Shoes, not Stockings, nor any thing else about me; whereas, had I been aware of such an Opportunity, but one quarter of an Hour before, I could have provided my self something better. However, thought I, if I can but once get footing on Terra-Firma, tho' in never so bad Circumstances, I shall call it a happy Deliverance; for I was resolved, come what would, never to come on board again."

When the longboat landed, Ashton was the most active worker of all in moving the heavy casks up on the beach. When the task was over he naturally went off by himself as if to rest, picking up stones and shells along the beach until he was quite a distance from the others. Then he walked toward the edge of the woods, whereupon the cooper called out to him, asking where he was going.

"I'm going to get some coconuts," Ashton replied. Soon he reached the forest and broke into a run, out of sight of the pirates. This daring act is so much like Stevenson's hero in

Treasure Island that it may be Ashton served as a model for that tale.

In the meantime the pirates had filled the water casks and were ready to return to the ship. Ashton huddled in the dense forest, burrowing into a thicket, while the cries sounded out around him, calling him back to the longboat. Ashton kept a discreet silence. After a long time the pirates gave up and rowed out to their ship. Philip Ashton was thus alone on a desolate, uninhabited island.

When he was sure the pirates had left, Ashton ventured from his hiding place to a spot down the beach about a mile from the watering place, where he could observe what went on aboard the pirate vessels. Five days later they sailed away, leaving him very much alone on the island.

> I began to reflect upon myself and my present Condition; I was upon an island from whence I could not get off; I knew of no Humane Creature within many scores of Miles of me; I had but a Scanty Cloathing, and no possibility of getting more; I was destitute of all Provision for my Support, and knew not how I should come at any; . . .

Ashton walked around the island, situated to the north of Cape Honduras in Central America, estimating it to be some thirty miles in length. There were no signs of human habitation. Later, however, Ashton located a great grove of lime trees and near them some broken fragments of earthen pots, from which he concluded Indians had formerly lived on the island.

Wild figs, grapes and coconuts were plentiful, but Ashton found no way of opening the coconut husks. Then he discovered an oval-shape fruit, larger than an orange, which was red inside and contained two or three stones slightly smaller than a walnut. Fearing he might be poisoned, Ashton kept away from them until one day he chanced upon a group of wild hogs devouring the fruit. This encouraged him to sample the fruit, which he found delicious. He called them "Mammees Supporters"; today they are known as papayas. Ashton discovered sundry other fruits and herbs, although he avoided the "Mangeneil Apple," which he claimed would have killed him.

Deer, wild hogs, lizards, ducks, "Teil," curlews, "Galdings," snakes, pelicans, boobies, pigeons and parrots, with tortoises along the beaches, made up the wildlife on the island of Roatan. Ashton could not take advantage of the situation, however, for he had no knife or weapon of any kind, and was without means of making a fire. But he did discover hundreds of tortoise eggs in nests on the beach, and grew very fond of this change in his fruit-and-vegetable diet. He became quite a naturalist in observing the habits of the tortoise, noticing that the creatures lay their eggs in the sand above the high-water mark, depositing them in a hollow twelve to eighteen inches deep. Then the tortoise fills the hole, and smooths over the sand. The eggs, Ashton found, usually hatch in eighteen to twenty days, after which the young turtles make a rush for the water.

The lizards were giants, as big around as "a Man's wast," and about twelve to fourteen feet long. Ashton's first encounter was a terrible experience, for he mistook it for a log, whereupon it opened its mouth wide enough "to have thrown a Hat into it, and blew out its Breath at me." There were smaller serpents on the island, some of them poisonous, especially a snake called the "Barber's Pole, being streaked White and Yellow. But I met with no Rattle-Snakes there, unless the Pirates," concluded Ashton.

The mosquitoes and flies bothered Ashton greatly, in particular the small black flies. He found that a certain key located off the island was free from all flies and insects. Being a poor swimmer, he constructed a bamboo life preserver to ensure his arriving safely at the island. With his frock and trousers bound to his head, he swam across, donning his clothes on reaching the island. Unfortunately he never was able to bring out enough wood or branches to construct a hut there, or he might have made the low, treeless key his permanent abode. His new home he called Day Island, his older residence Night Island.

One time, just as he left the deep water while swimming to Day Island, he was severely struck from behind. To his astonishment the culprit was a huge shovel-nosed shark, grounded in the shallow water and thus not able to seize him. Ashton became a more and more experienced swimmer, but he never forgot that narrow escape from death.

The greatest trial Ashton had to endure was the lack of shoes. His bare feet soon were masses of ugly bruises and cuts from the sticks and stones away from the beach and the sharp shell fragments on the shore. Although he walked along as tenderly as he could, he would frequently step on a sharp rock or shell, which would "run into the Old Wounds & the Anguish of it would strike me down as suddenly as if I had been shot thro', & oblige me to set down and Weep by the hour together at the extremity of my Pain."

At one time he fell ill and was attacked by one of the wild boars. Managing to climb partway up a tree, Ashton felt the tusks of the boar as they ripped through his clothing and tore away a substantial section of the cloth. The boar then left the scene. This was the only time a wild beast bothered him in any way, but it almost proved fatal.

Growing worse instead of better, Ashton despaired of life itself. In his sickness and unhappiness, he longed for the sight of his parents.

The rains began during October and continued for five months. Throughout this time the air was raw and cold, similar to a New England northeasterly storm. During these months he wished for fire but was never able to produce it while alone on the island.

An amazing incident took place in November 1723, when Ashton sighted a craft approaching him in the distance. As it drew closer he could see it was a canoe, with one man paddling. Ashton, very feeble at the time, made no effort to conceal himself. The canoeist paddled close to shore and observed Ashton at the edge of the beach. Shouting to the Marblehead sailor, the canoeist asked who he was and what he was doing. After Ashton told his story, the stranger, whose name Ashton never found out, came ashore and shook hands with the sick islander.

It was a happy occasion for poor Philip Ashton when he could actually see and talk with another human being. The man, who was English, had been living with the Spaniards for the last twenty-two years, but for some undisclosed reason they decided to burn him alive and he fled to Roatan Island.

Building a fire—he had tongs and a flint—the Englishman told the sick Marbleheader that he would paddle out and hunt venison for him, planning to return in a few days. He gave Ashton his knife, the tongs and flint, five pounds of pork and a bottle of powder before departing three days later.

Ashton never saw him again. Within an hour after the canoe disappeared in the distance, a terrific storm hit the island, probably drowning the Englishman at sea. A canoe drifted ashore some time later, but after careful examination Ashton decided it was not that of the Britisher.

With the aid of the tools and implements his friend had given him, Philip Ashton was soon eating a more balanced diet, and the fire kept him comfortable during the bad weather. Slowly regaining his strength, he would walk along the beach, watching the crabs in the shallow water. Ashton finally developed a manner of catching them at night, by lighting a torch and wading waist deep with it in the water. The crabs, attracted by the light, would hasten to it, whereupon Ashton would spear them with a sharpened stick he carried in his other hand.

Growing stronger daily, Ashton made plans that involved the canoe he had found on the beach. He then thought himself "Admiral of the Neighbouring Seas," and decided to make a tour of some of the more distant islands. Storing up a supply of grapes, figs, tortoise and other eatables, with his precious flint box safely packed away, he set out for the island of Bonaca, some six leagues westward.

Approaching the distant land, Ashton noticed a sloop off the eastern shore. He pulled his craft up on the beach at the western end of Bonaca. He walked overland to the other side of the island but could not make out the sloop. Tired from his journey, he sat down at the foot of a large tree near the shore and went to sleep.

Suddenly awakened by gunfire, he jumped to his feet to find nine large canoes, filled with Spaniards, coming up on the beach in front of him, with several of the men discharging their guns at him. He ran for the nearest thicket, whereupon they all landed and went after him. But he was adept at concealing himself by this time. After searching for several hours, the Spanish sailors paddled away from the vicinity and Ashton went down to the shore. He noticed the tree where he had fallen asleep, and saw several bullet holes uncomfortably near where his head had been. It took him three days to return to his canoe, for his rush into the thicket had opened up old wounds. He found the canoe undisturbed and was soon paddling away from the island. His experiences while there made him eager to return to Roatan, which he reached without incident.

Seven long months passed. Finally, in June 1724, when he was out on his Day Island off the shore, two large canoes approached. The men aboard noticed the smoke from Ashton's fire. Ashton at once fled to the Night Island in his canoe.

Glancing back, he saw that the canoes were slowly following ashore, indicating that they were as afraid of Ashton as he was of them.

Observing their extreme caution, Ashton decided they could not be pirates. He went openly down to the shore to find out what he could. The visitors leaned back on their oars and paddles and asked Ashton who he was.

> I told them I was an English Man, and had Run away from the Pirates. Upon this they drew something nearer and enquired who was there besides my self; I assured them I was alone. . . . They told me they were Bay-men, come from the Bay [Honduras]. This was comfortable News to me; so I bid them pull ashoar, there was no danger.

They first sent one man ashore, whom Ashton went down to meet. When the visitor saw such a "Poor, Ragged, Lean, Wan, Forlorn, Wild, Miserable, Object so near him" he started back, frightened from the shock. On recovering, he shook hands with Ashton, who embraced him with joy. Then the sailor picked poor Ashton up in his arms and carried him down to the canoes, where the entire company soon surrounded him in wonderment.

When Ashton told them he had been living on the island for sixteen months, the group was amazed. After they gave him a small amount of rum, he fell down insensible, overcome by the effects of the drink to which he was unaccustomed. But he revived slowly and later was as well as could be expected.

The Bay men told him that they had fled from the Spaniards, who, they feared, were about to assault them. They soon moved everything ashore, and within a short time had erected a substantial dwelling a little distance away on one of the windswept keys. They named this new home the Castle of Comfort. Ashton recovered his strength and spirits aided by the presence of so many human beings around him, and was soon joining in hunting expeditions. He made a good friend of an old man the Bay men called Father Hope, who told him of his many experiences, finally revealing that he had buried a small treasure chest in the woods.

Six months later pirates appeared. Ashton had gone over to Bonaca to hunt with three other men. Returning one night to Roatan Island, they were surprised at the sound of heavy firing. Coming into the moonlit harbor, they noticed that a large vessel was besieging the "Castle of Comfort." Taking down their sail as rapidly as possible, the four islanders rowed out of the harbor. Unfortunately, they had been detected. Soon a canoe with eight or ten men was chasing them. Drawing closer to the fleeing men, the invaders discharged a swivel gun mounted in the bow of the canoe. The shot landed in the water ahead.

The attacking party were actually pirates from Spriggs's vessel, the same from which Ashton had escaped. Reaching shore before the buccaneers could catch them, the islanders fled into the woods. The disappointed pirates landed on the beach, taking the canoe that the men had left on the shore, and then departed from the island. Ashton described what happened when his friends surrendered:

> Accordingly they took all the Men ashoar, and with them an Indian Woman and Child; those of them that were ashoar abused the Woman shamefully. They killed one Man after they were come ashoar, and threw him into one of the Baymens Canoes, where their Tar was, and set Fire to it, and burnt him in it. Then they carried our People on Board their Vessels, where they were barbarously treated.

Learning of treasure in the woods that had been hidden by old Father Hope, the pirates beat Hope unmercifully until he revealed the location. They found the treasure and took it away with them. Before leaving, the pirates gave the Bay men a craft of about five tons in which to sail to the Bay, but made them promise not to communicate with Ashton or his group. Then the pirates sailed away for good.

Father Hope decided a bad promise was better broken than kept, so came at once to the hiding place of Ashton and his friends. A conference was held on plans for the future. All except Ashton, John Symonds and a slave belonging to Symonds wished to leave at once for the Bay. Ashton at first was tempted to go, but decided that the chances for a ship were better at the island. Farewells were made, and the Bay men left in their small craft.

The season was now approaching for the Jamaica traders to sail in the vicinity. Because Bonaca was a favorite watering place for the traders, the three men went there. On the fifth day a great storm came up, which blew hard for three days. When the worst of the gale had passed, Ashton noticed a large fleet of vessels standing for the island's harbor. The larger vessels anchored off, but a brigantine came in over the shoals, making for the watering place. Three Englishmen, as Ashton could tell by their dress, rowed a longboat to shore. Ashton ran down to the beach.

Seeing the queer apparition, the men stopped rowing and asked Ashton who he was. He joyfully answered, "An Englishman run away from pirates!" They were satisfied and came to the beach. Ashton soon found that the ships were the British man-of-war *Diamond,* with a fleet of traders in convoy, bound to Jamaica, and that they were ashore to get fresh water because many sailors were very sick aboard ship. After a short time Mr. Symonds showed himself. He had been careful to keep out of sight for fear of alarming the sailors.

The brigantine proved to be from Salem, Massachusetts, less than three miles from Ashton's home. The master of the brig, Captain Dove, was shorthanded and signed Ashton on at once. It was a sad farewell with Symonds a few days later, but as Ashton said, "I was forced to go thro' for the Joy of getting Home."

One can imagine the thoughts that passed through Ashton's mind on the sail up through the Gulf of Florida, and finally the thrill when the brigantine first came abeam of Halfway Rock and headed for the passageway between Baker's Island and the Miseries in Boston Bay. He had been away from home two years, ten months and fifteen days. As soon as the ship landed, he journeyed at once to his home in Marblehead. His family, which had long ago given him up for lost, joyously greeted him.

Thus ends the remarkable story of Philip Ashton. When he recovered his health and strength, Ashton related his experiences to the Reverend John Barnard, who had preached a timely sermon in honor of the boy's return, choosing as his text "God's Ability to Save His People from All Danger."

CHAPTER 3

Edward Teach,
Alias Blackbeard

Edward Teach, alias Blackbeard, was born in Bristol, England, although the exact location of his birthplace is unknown. Going to sea at an early age, Teach did not attract attention until 1716, when he was serving under pirate Benjamin Thornigold. Early the next year Captain Thornigold, with Teach aboard, sailed from New Providence in the West Indies for the American mainland, capturing several vessels in rapid succession, including a Havana sloop with 120 barrels of flour and a ship loaded with wine from Bermuda. Next a craft from Madeira, loaded with a rich cargo of silks and bullion, was intercepted and robbed, after which the vessel was allowed to proceed to her South Carolina destination.

Their next capture was a large French guineaman bound for Martinique. By this time Edward Teach had shown such energy and leadership that he asked Captain Thornigold if he could take charge of the latest capture. Thornigold agreed, and Captain Edward Teach began a piratical career of his own. Because of the King's proclamation offering pardon to all pirates who would reform, Captain Thornigold soon returned to New Providence, where he surrendered to the mercy of the government there.

Teach soon had forty sizable guns, most from recent captures, mounted on board his vessel. He named the craft the *Queen Anne's Revenge.* Near the island of Saint Vincent he fell in with the *Great Allan,* commanded by Captain Christopher Taylor. A thorough job of pilfering was done on this fine vessel, with all valuable supplies removed to the pirate sloop. The crew members of the *Great Allan* were put ashore at Saint Vincent and the ship set afire.

An event now occurred which put Teach on a special pedestal in the annals of piracy. Falling in with the British man-of-war *Scarborough,* of thirty guns, Blackbeard successfully fought the English warship for several hours while blood flowed freely on the decks of both ships. The Britisher withdrew and ran for the nearest harbor in Barbados. Pleased with his defeat of the English warship, Captain Teach sailed triumphantly for Spanish America, with his fame as a bold and dangerous pirate spreading rapidly around the blue waters of the Atlantic Ocean.

Shortly afterward he fell in with a Major Stede Bonnet, an interesting pirate who had formerly been a gentleman of good reputation and estate on the island of Barbados. This man had taken up piracy for excitement and adventure. Unfortunately for Bonnet, however, he knew nothing of navigation, so Blackbeard tactfully suggested that the major come aboard the *Queen Anne's Revenge* to serve as Teach's lieutenant, while Teach would send an experienced master aboard Bonnet's own sloop, the *Revenge.*

"As you have not been used to the fatigues and cares of such a post," said Teach to Bonnet, "it would be better for you to decline it and live easy, at your pleasure, in such a ship as mine, where you will not be obliged to perform duty, but follow your own inclinations." Major Bonnet quickly saw the wisdom of Teach's statement and exchanged places with pirate Richards, who took charge of the Bonnet sloop.

A short time later the pirates were loading fresh water at Turneffe, near the Bay of Honduras, when they saw a sloop enter the inlet. Captain Richards, hoisting the black flag of piracy, slipped his cable and ran out to encounter the stranger. The sloop was the *Adventure,* commanded by Captain David Harriot, who observed the black pirate flag on Richard's mast and ordered his own sails struck at once, finally coming to under the stern of the *Queen Anne's Revenge.* Harriot and his crew were quickly transferred to the larger vessel. Israel Hands, whose name Robert Louis Stevenson borrowed for one of his pirates in *Treasure Island,* was given command of the *Adventure.*

On April 9, 1717, the pirate fleet weighed anchor and left Turneffe for the Bay of Honduras. Here they found a ship and four sloops. The ship was the *Protestant Caesar,* out of Boston, commanded by Captain Wyar. When Teach hoisted his pirate flag and fired his gun, Captain Wyar and every member of his crew fled ashore in their boat. The four sloops were quickly captured, whereupon the *Caesar* was ransacked and set afire, along with one of the sloops. Teach explained that the two vessels were destroyed because they came from Boston, where the inhabitants had had the unmitigated nerve to hang certain captured pirates.

Some time later the sea rovers, cruising in waters around Grand Cayman, about sixty miles westward of Jamaica, seized a small craft occupied in hunting turtles, which abounded in the waters nearby. Working northward toward the Carolinas on the Atlantic coast, they engaged and captured three more vessels. Soon the buccaneers sighted the shores of the North American mainland.

Off the bar at Charles-Town, or Charleston as it is known today, they waited several days until a ship came out. It was a vessel bound for London, commanded by Captain Robert

Clark. The pirates took it in short order. The following day four more captures were made: a ship, a brigantine and two pinkies. All the prisoners were herded aboard the pirate vessels. This activity threw terror into the hearts of the inhabitants of Charleston.

At this time there were eight sails in Charleston harbor, none of which dared go out and risk capture by Blackbeard. Word also reached other ports that the notorious Edward Teach was near Charleston harbor, so incoming commerce as well was suspended. It was a particularly trying period for the colonists of South Carolina, who had just finished a grueling war with the Tuscarora Indians.

Every ship and every man taken by Teach had been detained off the bar. Now Blackbeard showed not only his colossal nerve but his contempt for Americans in general. He sent his representative, Captain Richards, right into the harbor and ashore in the center of town, with a message demanding a chest of medicine for the pirate fleet. Teach could afford to be insolent, for aboard his ship as a prisoner was Samuel Bragg, one of the governor's councilmen. Richards told the people of Charleston that unless they sent the chest of medicine out to the fleet, all the prisoners would be murdered and every ship set afire. Richards and the other two pirates strutted through the streets of Charleston, appearing wherever and whenever they wished.

The governor soon reached a decision with his councilmen. Since there was nothing else they could do but comply with Blackbeard's wishes, the citizens of Charleston sent the pirate fleet an expensive chest of medicine worth at least three hundred pounds. When Teach received the chest, he kept his word and freed every prisoner after he had robbed them of their wealth, which totaled 1500 pounds in gold and silver.

North Carolina was now the destination of the pirate fleet, which consisted of Teach's "man-of-war," two "privateers" and a small sloop serving as a tender. The pirate captain soon broke up his company, cheating and marooning those for whom he did not care and dividing the spoils with his friends.

About this time Teach decided to take advantage of the proclamation of His Majesty granting a "gracious pardon to those guilty of acts of piracy who would surrender themselves to the authorities on or before a certain date." He visited the governor to obtain a certificate of his desire to retire from the pirating profession. Then followed a shameful act by Governor Charles Eden, who ordered a court of Vice-Admiralty held at Bath-Town for the purpose of declaring Teach an honest privateer. This farce of justice was carried through according to law, thus enabling Blackbeard to lay claim to a vessel he had captured from the Spanish some time before, although England and Spain were not at war when the capture was made.

Before Captain Teach left Bath-Town he fell in love with a girl of fifteen. He asked Governor Eden to officiate at the marriage, although the pirate's marital life was a trifle overcrowded: he had thirteen wives. The governor readily performed the ceremony, after which Blackbeard moved for a few days to the plantation of his new wife's family. The girl's happiness was short-lived, for Blackbeard invited his ruffian friends out to the plantation, where they all caroused, gambled and drank night after night. It was not long before the poor girl was totally miserable. Much to her relief, Teach sailed away shortly afterward. Tradition has it that the pirates went far to the north on this particular voyage, running in at the Isles of Shoals off the New Hampshire coast.

According to legend, Blackbeard often went ashore at the Isles of Shoals, having as his special abode Smuttynose Island. After a trip to England he returned to the islands with a woman whom he took ashore. A considerable portion of Blackbeard's silver treasure was buried at this time. Telling the girl to guard the treasure until his return, Teach sailed away with his pirate band but never came back, continuing his career elsewhere. There she lived for many years and finally died on this lonely island. It was said her ghost haunted the Isles of Shoals for almost a century. Regardless of the truth of the story, there is no question that Samuel Haley, in building a wall many years later, uncovered four bars of solid silver worth a fortune. Haley built a breakwater between his property and the adjoining island at Malaga after the discovery of the fortune, and many believe that part of the money he used was from Blackbeard's treasure.

Teach sailed for Bermuda in June 1718. Falling in with three English vessels, he took from them only such food and provisions as he needed. Shortly afterward he came upon two French sloops bound for Martinique. He put both French crews aboard one vessel, which he permitted to go free. Teach sailed the second ship to North Carolina, where he and the governor shared the spoils. Governor Charles Eden demanded that everything should be done legally, and so he had Teach swear that he found the French ship adrift at sea. The governor then convened a court that declared the vessel condemned. This action allowed Governor Eden to have sixty hogsheads of sugar as his share; the governor's secretary, Mr. Knight, received twenty barrels for his efforts. The pirates were permitted to have the rest of the cargo, but the ship remained in the harbor, causing Teach a great deal of worry. He was afraid that other vessels might recognize her, so he told the governor the ship was leaking and might sink, blocking the inlet. Thereupon Governor Eden ordered Teach to sail her out, giving Blackbeard the opportunity to burn her to the water's edge and sink the vessel in deep water.

Records of some of the strange incidents aboard Blackbeard's ship have been preserved. One night Teach sat drinking in the cabin with Israel Hands and another man. Suddenly he drew out two pistols and cocked them under the table. The other pirate observed what was going on and quickly left the cabin, but Hands did not notice Teach's action. Blackbeard suddenly blew out the candle, crossed his hands under the table, and fired. Israel Hands received the full force of one of the pistols in his knee, leaving him lame for the rest of his life. Some time later other members of the crew asked Blackbeard why he had injured one of his good friends. "If I do not now and then kill one of you, you'll forget who I am," was the astonishing reply.

Teach's beard was the talk of two continents. Jet black, it completely covered his face, even growing around his eyes, giving him a fierce appearance that he made the most of. He would twist the ends into small pigtails, fastening them with hair ribbons and turning them about his ears. When going into battle he purposely tried to create an effect to overwhelm his adversaries with fear, wearing three braces of pistols hanging in holsters from his shoulders. Inserting hemp cord under his hat, Blackbeard would set the hemp ends afire to burn like punk, making his eyes look fierce and wild. His whole appearance suggested the Devil himself.

There was one man who had heard of the notorious buccaneer Edward Teach and had determined to end the career of this monster who preyed on shipping up and down the coast. He was Lieutenant Robert Maynard of the British man-of-war *Pearl*. Maynard was thoroughly exasperated by the fear Blackbeard created among some of the inhabitants of North Carolina and the tolerance with which he was treated by others.

A group of planters and traders of the North Carolina coast, also deciding that they had had enough of the deprivations of Blackbeard, met together secretly to plan a campaign of retaliation. Knowing that their governor was hand in hand with Teach, they expected no help from him and so decided to send a delegation of protest direct to Virginia.

Governor Alexander Spotswood of Virginia received the

North Carolina planters with courtesy and kindness. He agreed that something must be done, and that it was useless to consult Governor Eden of North Carolina. It was arranged that two small sloops should be hired, capable of running over the shoals where buccaneer Teach was lurking. It was also agreed that they should be manned by two crews chosen from the man-of-war vessels *Pearl* and *Lime,* then at anchor in the James River. The command of the expedition was given to pirate-hating Robert Maynard.

As the two sloops were made fit for sea, Governor Spotswood called an assembly, which agreed with him on the actions to be taken. Of course, the Virginia governor must have realized that he had not the slightest jurisdiction over North Carolina, which he mentioned in his proclamation. But he probably decided that the legal sidestep was necessary because of the gravity of the situation. And he was right.

Lieutenant Maynard lost no time getting the expedition ready for sea. Sailing from Kicquetan, on the James River, the two vessels had reached the mouth of Ocracoke Inlet when the spars and masts of Teach's vessel were sighted. Although the proclamation had not been officially issued at the time Maynard arrived off the inlet, Mr. Knight of North Carolina, who had spies in Virginia, had already written to Blackbeard, warning him of trouble brewing. When Blackbeard saw the sloops approaching, he stripped his vessel for action, and awaited his adversaries.

By the time Maynard reached the vicinity of the pirate stronghold, darkness was falling. Maynard wisely anchored for the night.

The channel was intricate, with many shoals. When morning came Maynard sent a boat ahead to sound, and followed slowly behind. Despite this precaution, the sloops grounded on several sandy spots. Maynard ordered all ballast thrown overboard.

Even the water barrels were emptied, for Maynard was determined to capture Blackbeard or die in the attempt.

Finally Blackbeard fired a shot in the direction of the two sloops, whereupon Maynard hoisted the King's colors and stood directly for Captain Teach's vessel. The pirate chieftain cut his cable, planning to make a running fight of it. The sloops were without cannon, while Teach could use his, giving the pirates a definite advantage at first. Maynard was not deterred in the least by this, proceeding with his plans as if all were in his favor. Finally the two opposing forces were close enough for hailing distance.

"Damn you for villains, who are you?" asked the exasperated pirate captain. "And from whence came you?"

"You may see by our colors we are no pirates," responded the resolute Maynard, who now felt fairly certain of his objective.

Blackbeard then asked Maynard to send his boat aboard, so he could find out who he was. But Maynard was not to be tricked. "I cannot spare my boat, but I will come aboard of you as soon as I can with my sloop," replied the British lieutenant.

This so upset Blackbeard that he went below to regain his composure. Returning to the deck, he glowered across at Maynard. "Damnation seize my soul if I give you quarter or take any from you," the thoroughly angered buccaneer declared.

"I do not expect quarter from you, nor shall I give any," replied Maynard. It is clear why Maynard was called a brave man. He was about to tackle one of the hardest fighting pirates the world has ever known, and had nothing but small arms while buccaneer Teach was armed with many cannon.

Blackbeard's sloop, which had run aground, was soon floated off in the incoming tide, but the wind died down completely. Afraid that his prey would escape, Maynard ordered his men to the sweeps, and in this manner he rapidly gained on the becalmed pirates. Suddenly Captain Teach let go with a broad-side, which did terrific slaughter to the poor men at the sweeps who were exposed as they were rowing. When the smoke of the discharge had cleared, it was discovered that no less than twenty-nine were either killed or wounded in Maynard's two sloops.

It was a serious blow to the English officer's plans. Many another equally brave leader would have given up then and there. Maynard, however, was determined to capture or kill the great Blackbeard and forever rid the seas of his presence. The British lieutenant ordered all hands below, remaining on deck alone with the man at the helm, whom he told to crouch down as far as possible. The other sloop was out of the contest, temporarily disabled by the broadside. The wind now freshened a trifle, allowing Maynard's sloop to draw closer to the pirates. But it was a difficult course, the sloop grounding and sliding off time and again.

Maynard ordered two ladders placed in the hatchway so that the men could scramble from the hold on signal. Closer and closer the sloop came to the pirates, who were awaiting them with hand grenades. When within throwing distance, the pirates lighted the short fuses on the grenades and tossed them over to the deck of the sloop. With most of the sailors below, the grenades exploded harmlessly.

When the smoke had partially cleared, Blackbeard looked over at the sloop. "They are all knocked on the head except three or four," he exclaimed. "Let's jump aboard and cut them to pieces."

As the two ships came together, Blackbeard and fourteen of the pirates jumped across to Maynard's vessel. Then the men belowdecks raced up the ladders and the bloody conflict began. The tides of victory surged back and forth, with sabers gleaming and flashing in the sun and the fatal charges from pistols echoing across the water. The two forces fought on until almost every man was bathed in blood.

Edward Teach, alias Blackbeard, was in his last fight, although he probably did not realize it. Anxious to come to blows with the British upstart who had threatened his piratical kingdom, he gradually worked his way aft until he could see Lieutenant Maynard. The brave British officer had also noticed the fearsome spectacle that he identified as Blackbeard, and was advancing to meet him. Having waited for such a long time to come to grips with this hated outlaw, who represented everything loathsome connected with the ocean, Maynard was not frightened by the truly dreadful apparition that came at him from the thinning smoke of gunshot and hand grenade.

Maynard and Blackbeard fired at each other simultaneously. Blackbeard missed while Maynard wounded his adversary in the body. Despite this, the huge, lumbering form kept moving steadily forward, suddenly striking with a terrific sweep of his cutlass, smashing into Maynard's sword with such force that it broke the weapon at the hilt. Regaining his balance for a fresh lunge to finish off the lieutenant, Blackbeard drew back his cutlass. As he started his second sweeping parabola, he was given a terrific blow in the throat by a British marine. This telling wound deflected his own blow so that it struck Maynard's knuckles instead of killing him.

The odds of the battle seemed to change time after time. Finally, when Blackbeard had suffered twenty saber thrusts and five pistol wounds, he was seen to waver. Just as he began to cock his last pistol, having fired three others previously, he was seized with a spasm. Tottering for a brief moment in helplessness, Blackbeard fell dead at the very feet of the man who had sworn to take him, Lieutenant Robert Maynard. By this time only a few of the buccaneers were left alive. When they saw that their leader was dead, they quickly jumped over the side into the water, crying for quarter. Maynard told them they could have mercy, but did not guarantee them from hanging later on.

Back on the pirate ship the sailors from Maynard's other sloop had finally gone into action. The outlaws aboard Teach's vessel, who had seen Blackbeard go down to death and defeat, also asked for mercy.

It had been a glorious but fearful day for the British officers and sailors. Lieutenant Maynard deserved all the credit for the victory, for he had pushed ahead in the face of what seemed hopeless defeat to win one of the greatest encounters ever staged with pirates along the Atlantic coast. His subsequent conduct in continuing the fight after twenty-nine of his small force had been put out of action showed the highest bravery.

Blackbeard's plans miscarried aboard his own vessel. Had not Teach believed victory was certain when he boarded the Maynard sloop, the pirate vessel would have been blown up, for Blackbeard left explicit orders to set off the gunpowder should defeat seem imminent. Apparently victory changed to disaster so rapidly and unexpectedly that the pirate charged with blowing up the ship if defeat threatened could not reach the powder magazine in time. Thus the outlaw vessel, with all its incriminating documents, was left secure for Maynard to go aboard and salvage. Among the documents Maynard found were many letters addressed to Teach from leading citizens in various colonies along the Atlantic coast.

After all had been secured, Maynard ordered Blackbeard's head severed from his neck and suspended from the bowsprit of the victorious sloop. In this manner Maynard sailed into Bath-Town, where he and his ship excited the awe and amazement of the entire populace. Sending his wounded men ashore for treatment, Maynard left at once for the governor's storehouse. Armed with the incriminating letters between Secretary Knight of Bath-Town and pirate Teach, involving twenty barrels of sugar for Knight and sixty for Governor Eden, Maynard boldly seized the eighty barrels piled up in the warehouse and ordered them taken away. Secretary Knight was so frightened that he actually fell sick with fear, literally scared to death by the consequences of his act and its discovery. He died a few days later.

With the ferocious head of the infamous Blackbeard still dangling from the end of the bowsprit, Maynard sailed out of Bath-Town and reached the James River, where the inspiring news of his daring exploit had preceded him. The sale of the pirate sloop and of certain pirate effects and supplies located ashore came to 2500 pounds, a tidy sum, in addition to the rewards paid for the apprehension of the pirates. All of this small fortune, the equivalent of well over $20,000 today, was given to the survivors of the battle aboard the *Pearl.*

The result of the trial held later in Virginia was a forgone conclusion, with two exceptions. Israel Hands, ashore at the time of capture, was later apprehended and brought to the bar, where he was convicted and sentenced to be hanged. Told of the extension of King George's proclamation, this condemned pirate in the shadow of the gallows had the cleverness to announce that he would agree to the King's offer and turn honest. The astonished justices in turn were forced to accept his statement as sincere, and pardoned him on the spot. Some years later pirate biographer Johnson heard that Hands had turned up in London, where he practiced for many years as a professional beggar.

Another pirate, Samuel Odell, was discovered to have been removed from a trading sloop the very night before the engagement. Having received no less than seventy wounds in the encounter, Odell was acquitted, and gratefully left the courtroom. He later recovered completely from his many injuries.

Nine of the pirates had been killed in the battle, with the two acquitted making eleven who were not hanged. All the other pirates, fourteen in number, were hanged with proper ceremony in the royal colony of Virginia. But the body of Captain Edward Teach, alias Blackbeard, did not grace any Virginia gibbet. This most ferocious pirate ended his career as he probably wished it would end, fighting a worthy opponent in the throes of a wild and thrilling conflict at sea.

PART TWO

Lighthouses

CHAPTER 1

The Flying Santa

The idea of a Flying Santa originated in 1927 with the late Captain Bill Wincapaw, who turned distribution of yuletide packages over to me in 1936. Since that time I have flown every year but one, 1942, when I was serving with the Air Corps. The Santa flights are not sponsored in any way, but voluntary contributions have helped considerably. Each year more than 90 percent of the flight cost is borne by me, and I have been more than repaid by the pleasure of seeing the waving lighthouse keepers and their families and by the letters they later send to me. My wife, Anna-Myrle, has gone on a majority of these flights, and our daughter, Dorothy, went each year until she was married.

The bundles contain balloons from Tillotson Rubber Company, Sevigny candy and lollipops, Gillette razors and blades, gum, pens and pencils, dolls, pocket edition books and a copy of my latest book. One year a friend gave doll clothes she had made, another sent socks and potholders, while others have sent money for cigarettes and children's toys. On occasion Girl Scout troops and women's church groups have contributed.

In the past we have at times invited our neighbors and friends to help wrap the bundles. After clearing the Ping-Pong table, we assign the various jobs: cutting twine and tying a bow-line on the end, opening newspapers for preliminary wrapping, arranging materials in an assembly line, checking the master list to see that everything is gathered, then the final packing.

Each gift is wrapped in newspapers. Excelsior is placed in a grocery bag before the gifts are put in, with more excelsior on top to form a cushion. Heavy wrapping paper next encases the gifts, with additional excelsior and then twine securely around the bundle. Finally there is a neat row of bundles ready to pack into the car and later into the plane.

More and more lighthouse keepers ask me to visit them. We have no regular route and have not tried to visit every light every year. But we have gone from the French possession of Saint Pierre and Miquelon, Sable Island off Nova Scotia and the Maine lighthouses down to Saint Augustine, Florida, and Bermuda. On one occasion we dropped a package at New York's Fire Island Light in the morning, then crossed the country to drop bundles at various light stations in California that evening. A card of acknowledgment from Fire Island Light, Bay Shore, Long Island, New York, said:

12-17-53

Dear Flying Santa,
    We have received your package. Many thanks, and a Merry Christmas to you and Happy Landings.

The Mahlers and Hodges

The next card we received was from California:

Point Vincente Light Station
Palos Verdes Estates, Calif.
December 17, 1953

Dear Mr. Santa Snow:
    We received the packages and thanks a lot for the

same. May the good Lord give you as much pleasure in delivering as we get in receiving. Once again we all thank both of you for your kindness. God Bless You.

Joseph Mary

In years past we have had a window in the airplane that could be opened to drop one, two or three packages at a lighthouse. Coming in low over the station, I let the package go just before the light flashes by, and the angle of approach allows the bundle to hit the target nineteen out of twenty times. Since airplane rules and regulations have become so strict, we have been forced to vary this in recent years.

Flying alone in the plane, chart before us to guide our approach and packages around us, excitement fills the cabin. Far in the distance we see a tiny shaft of white. For example, on one occasion we picked up the Isles of Shoals Light from a point over Gloucester, climbed for five minutes and started on our long gliding approach. First we buzzed the tower to alert the keeper, then came back to drop our bundle. For that brief moment the plane, the lighthouse and the package were all that really mattered. Then on a tight turn we came back over the tower to see legs running as fast as they could to retrieve the bundle and hold it up with a gesture of thanks.

One Sunday in 1940 I dropped Keeper Marden a package in Marblehead. He was in church, and his neighbors saw a car stop near where the bundle had hit. A man jumped out, swooped up the parcel and drove away rapidly. The next year I determined that the incident should not be repeated. Coming in less than one hundred feet in the air, I dropped the package at exactly the right moment and watched it thud on top of his roof and roll off to the ground. Keeper Marden, equal to the occasion, wrote to me the following day: "I received your package which arrived in good order, landing on the roof. Thank God it wasn't a bomb."

Captain Veidler was keeper at Nauset Beach Light, Cape Cod, during the 1940s. In 1943 he prepared an unusual greeting for me when I flew over Nauset Light with his Christmas parcel. As we banked over the lighthouse, I noticed that a welcome had been spelled out in the area just behind the building. The greeting, SANTA HELLO, was formed with scrub pine branches. Keeper Veidler, his son and his wife had worked all morning arranging the boughs so that we could read the words from the air.

Keeper Bakken and his wife put up their Christmas tree and waited to decorate it until the Santa package arrived at their station at Cape Porpoise Light on Goat Island, Maine. As soon as the plane zoomed in, dropped the gifts and left, the three children and the keeper rushed out to retrieve it. They put the wrapped gifts around the tree and perched the toy airplane at the very top. On Christmas morning the children were up early to open their gifts from the Flying Santa.

Many years ago I received a letter from five-year-old Seamond Ponsart of Cuttyhunk in the Elizabeth Islands. Seamond wanted the Flying Santa to drop her a doll. Santa complied, but Cuttyhunk Island is covered with huge boulders, and the doll smashed. As a result the broken-hearted little girl cried herself to sleep that night. The following year Keeper Ponsart moved his family to West Chop Light on Martha's Vineyard. I decided to deliver my gifts at that time by helicopter and was able to present her the doll in person. The trip was successful, and Seamond went to bed happy that night. Each year I receive a gift or a card from Seamond, who has been married and is now a member of the Coast Guard in New Orleans. I kept the first thank-you card sent by her parents long ago:

We have received your package and thank you very much. Seamond likes her doll and went to bed with it very

It was not until the following spring that I was able to journey by boat out to Graves Light, and we had quite a chat concerning the packages.

"Yes," admonished Reamy, "you made me row almost a mile to recover your bundle. A poor shot, I'd call it."

I explained that I had returned with another bundle, which I had dropped successfully. But he refused to believe me.

"Well," I cried, "let's go down and look."

The storms and waves had swept the ledge scores of times since I had dropped the parcel, but when I found the weather-beaten package, the articles could still be identified. The pen and pencil set had rusted, the cigars and cigarettes were soggy, the book pages were stuck together, the candy was ruined. Everything was completely spoiled, with one exception: the Gillette razor blades. The keeper carried these away in triumph and used them that very night.

Then there is the remarkable tale of the Flying Santa bundle dropped at Whaleback Light many years ago. I watched it become one of my more outstanding failures as it hit the sea at least forty feet from the lighthouse. After releasing another, we flew on our way.

That was December 18. On January 5, Colonel Eugene S. Clark, eminent marine expert of Sandwich, Massachusetts, was hiking along the Cape Cod beach after a storm. He saw something wrapped in brownish paper floating toward the shore. Retrieving the bundle, he found that it was the package I had dropped almost three weeks before at Whaleback Ledge. The bundle had floated across Massachusetts Bay to land in front of him on the Cape Cod beach, ninety miles in a direct line. The last I knew, he still had my book he found in the package, *Storms and Shipwrecks of New England,* now out of print.

Some years ago I released a package at Eastern Point Light, Gloucester. The keeper was watching the plane maneuver as I much pleased with her Santa. . . . She was also pleased with the other things in the package and also the rest of us. Come and visit when you can. . . . West Chop Light

—O. J. Ponsart, Keeper

Some years ago we were out over Boon Island. Swooping in low, the red twin-engined plane was barely fifty feet over the rocky ledges when I released the first aerial Christmas bomb, followed a moment later by another. The first landed successfully. But the second, to our surprise and horror, did something no package before or since has ever done: it became caught in the tail's elevator horn and completely locked the tail mechanism. Portsmouth, New Hampshire, was the nearest airport, and we landed there safely. Jumping to the runway, I walked back to the tail assembly while everyone at the airport ran out to see what had happened. The discovery of a Christmas package wedged in the tail made us realize what a narrow escape we had had.

On another occasion I threw a package out at far-flung Graves Light. We watched hopefully as the bundle dropped away from the plane, spinning down lower and lower, until finally it struck the riprap ledge near the tower and plopped into the sea. I had failed.

While we were making our cloverleaf turn, Keeper Reamy, who had watched from inside the tower as the parcel hit the ledge and then the water, was descending the metal stairs and could neither hear nor see us as we returned.

Back over the tower one minute later, I dropped a second bundle and watched it lodge safely in a cleft of the rocks. However, the keeper, unaware of what had happened, never did find it. Instead, he launched his dory into the teeth of a twenty-mile-an-hour gale and rowed desperately for forty minutes before retrieving the first package.

dropped the bundle but, because of our speed, it was hard to follow closely. The package landed safely, lodged in a rocky cleft, and on we flew. The following summer we visited the keeper, who refused to believe I had dropped anything for him as he had never found it.

The next year I made it a point to direct the bundles in plain view of the keeper. I telephoned to make certain he had received the three I dropped him. That August, twenty months after I dropped the package he said I had not left for him, my phone rang.

"Well, Mr. Snow," said the keeper of Eastern Point Light, "I've just been given the long-missing package. Some boys found it down near the rocks in a little cavity. It was wedged there securely. I must apologize for doubting you in the first place."

At times requests come for the Flying Santa. The Stockbridges of Burnt Island Light in Boothbay harbor, Maine, wrote: "This is our last Christmas at the Lighthouse, and we would so much like to see the Flying Santa for the last time. Happy landings and good luck and do save time to be at your own home during the holiday."

> Ram Island Light
> Boothbay harbor, Maine

Dear Mr. Edward Rowe Snow:

All of us will be watching for your plane, my husband Keeper Wendell J. Reece, my uncle Henry F. Knightley, my German Shepherd Rocky IV, my three little kittens and myself.

> Mrs. Tessie M. Reece

A special package was made for the Reeces, including dog biscuits. A telephone call that night assured us that the bundle had landed safely and that Rocky IV was already enjoying his present.

Two interesting incidents connected with the Santa bombing occurred at Ipswich Light years ago. One package landed inside the open door of the keeper's garage and was there waiting for him when he returned home. On another occasion the keeper was working in the cellar of his house. He had invited a group of children to a party to be held directly after the dropping of the bundle. The hour approached when the plane should make its appearance, so the keeper called out to his wife, "Has Santa arrived yet, dear?"

Before the lady could reply there was a terrific crash upstairs, and the bundle came hurtling along the upper hall after its surprising entrance through the skylight. His wife was equal to the occasion, and quickly answered without a tremor in her voice: "Yes, dear. We can start the party now."

We often visited Keeper Hopkins and his wife and son at their Ten Pound Island home, and found them a happy family. One Christmas week when I was about to take off from the East Boston Airport on the annual Christmas flight over the lighthouses, Mrs. Hopkins heard about it over the radio.

"Let's do something special for Ed Snow when he comes over," she suggested to her husband.

"What can we do?" he asked, and went back to reading a magazine story.

Mrs. Hopkins disappeared down the cellar stairs, coming up a short time later with her arms full of old newspapers. These she spread on the lawn beside the house to form the words MERRY CHRISTMAS. Then she nailed the papers to the ground so that the wind would not rearrange them.

An hour later I circled the island and was thrilled to read her greeting spelled out in the grass. A picture was taken, and when we returned to Boston later that day, it was processed by the

Associated Press. On the front pages of some of the late afternoon papers was that view of the greeting to the Flying Santa. Keeper Hopkins's son, returning home from school, purchased a copy of one of the Boston papers. He rowed out to the island and entered the kitchen, where his father was still sitting in his favorite chair, deep in a magazine. The son handed Hopkins the paper, holding it open to the four-column aerial picture of his own lighthouse and home, with the words MERRY CHRISTMAS in the grass.

His good wife continued to tell her story for many years, how she put one over on her husband by arranging the welcome for the Flying Santa.

One year at North Light, Block Island, Keeper John Lee had been shopping in Providence the week before Christmas and had purchased my latest book. In a day or two the same volume arrived as a present from a relative. Then when I flew over and dropped my package, another identical book was enclosed. In the letter of acknowledgment I received from John Lee, he told me what had happened. I mailed him another of my books with a different title.

The largest number of books I ever gave during the Flying Santa trips was four hundred pocket edition volumes, which I left at far-flung Sable Island in 1954. The bundles and books were fully appreciated by the children and grown-ups on this strange sand island of shipwrecks and wild horses.

At Baker's Island one year they had a HELLO SANTA greeting for us made out of driftwood, which the keeper collected on the beach and laid out to form letters in the snow near the lighthouse.

At Minot's Light, before the beacon was made automatic, we had to tie two or even three packages together with rope twenty feet long, arranged in a sort of meshing, so that when I released them they floated down and spread out to catch on one of the upper platforms of the tower. Nevertheless, as often as not they came down in the sea.

When two packages landed in the water on a blustery day at Ten Pound Island, Gloucester harbor, we thought they were lost. We did not know that the dog on the island, a retriever, swam out and brought the bundles ashore in good condition.

At Chatham Light an unusual incident took place. The keeper's card explains:

> We have received your package. Appreciated by all hands, excluding the broken windshield.
>   Mahlon A. Chase BMC OIC
>   Coast Guard Station
>   Chatham, Mass.

It seems that my aim was too good and the bundle went through the windshield of the car.

Here are a few more replies to the Flying Santa:

> As you well know the life of a light keeper at its very best is very lonely, and it gives one a good feeling to think that someone of your status would remember us on Christmas Day. I have been in the Coast Guard 21 years. . . . Again thank you very much.
>   Lyman D. Beach, BMC, USCG
>   Light Station, Mount Desert Rock

> Recovered 3 packages, one was water soaked and spoiled, one was wet and somewhat broken, and one was dry and in good condition. Thanks heaps. Good Luck.
>   Ram Island Light
>   Boothbay harbor, Maine

You will never know how much your thoughts made happier a routine lonely holiday away from home. This is about the only day that will get to a man out here on these stations. So well do I know as I spent 2 of them on lights on the west coast. With kind thoughts from people like you it still seems worthwhile. It was wonderful.

> Robert L. Zoner OIC
> Officer in Charge
> Seguin Light Station
> USCG

Just took over this duty. Was surprised and pleased to find the package. Thank you.

> T. H. Brown, BMC, USCG
> Race Point Light

One Coastguardsman, R. E. Morong, wrote thanking the Flying Santa and said that he could remember when he was a "lad of eleven when my Dad was stationed at Race Point Light Station, the fun we had looking for the packages that you dropped from the plane. It was a big event in our life."

In 1969 we stopped at the Rockland Airport, where several members of the Coast Guard and their families greeted us. Kenneth Black, at the time commanding officer of the Rockland Coast Guard Station, surprised the Flying Santa with a lamp presented on behalf of the members of the station. We distributed packages to the personnel along with balloons, candy, razors and books to the families there.

In the plane coming in from Rockland's Owl's Head, we can make out the almost perfect lighthouse setting of Curtis Island off Camden, Maine. Circling this beautiful isle makes me think of the thousands of people who have watched the movies we have made year after year from the plane.

Two years ago I did something I always wanted to attempt. Going on the Flying Santa trip by helicopter, I was able to stop at the lighthouses and meet the families of the Coast Guardsmen tending the lights. Several of the score of places where I landed are the Isles of Shoals, Seguin, Gloucester's Eastern Point and Cape Porpoise Light.

This reply card is typical of the many sent to us over the years:

> We have received your package. Thank you so much. We have a little boy who will be a year old tomorrow. He'll just love the balloons and punch ball. We've only been here two weeks, so you've certainly brightened our Christmas.
>
> Mr. and Mrs. C. E. Trebilcock
> Wood Island Light Station
> Biddeford Pool, Maine

CHAPTER 2

An American Army of Two

Attached to the old Scituate Lighthouse is a tablet bearing the words:

SCITUATE LIGHT HOUSE / BUILT 1810 / LIGHTED 1811
SIMEON BATES, REUBEN BATES, JAMES YOUNG BATES,
KEEPERS
REBECCA AND ABIGAIL BATES, DAUGHTERS OF SIMEON,
CALLED
"THE AMERICAN ARMY OF TWO"
PLACED BY THE BATES ASSOCIATION INC. 1928

It is unfortunate that a controversy still rages about the names of the two little heroines and what they did. Some claim that the whole story is a fabrication, but evidence indicates otherwise.

The usually accepted version of this interesting tale is that Reuben Bates,* the keeper at Scituate Light during the War of 1812, had two young daughters, Rebecca and Abigail, who were anxious and willing to help their country against the British. In the spring of 1814 the English man-of-war *Bulwark* lay at anchor off Scituate harbor. Keeper Bates feared that his light-

---

*As the years have gone by, the names of Reuben and Simeon have become interchanged, and there is no way of settling the matter at this late moment.

house would meet a fate similar to that experienced by Boston Light during the Revolution, when the upper works of America's oldest beacon were blown to pieces. But the British did not molest Scituate Light. On June 11, 1814, however, when the citizens of Scituate refused to furnish fresh meat and vegetables to the men on the *Bulwark,* two English barges were sent into the harbor itself, where the British marines set fires that destroyed many American boats and schooners.

Later in the summer a regiment from Boston under the command of Colonel John Barstow arrived in the vicinity, and the *Bulwark* soon left Scituate harbor. As the summer weeks passed without incident, discipline among the American soldiers was relaxed, so that the guards were visiting the village and combining pleasant diversions with their daily tasks.

One day early in September the British man-of-war *La Hogue* appeared off the coast when there were no guards at Scituate Lighthouse. Only the eldest daughter of Keeper Reuben Bates, fourteen-year-old Rebecca, her younger sister Abigail and a younger brother were at the light. Rebecca, high in the tower when she sighted the *La Hogue,* sent her brother off to the village to warn the people. Then she went down on the beach to plan what could be done. She watched the powerful warship tack and stand off to sea, then tack again and make for the harbor. The tide turned and began to come into the bay. It was a fine day, and a gentle breeze slightly ruffled the water as the *La Hogue* sailed nearer and nearer.

When high water came at two that afternoon, the man-of-war let go her bowers, swung her yards around and lay quiet in the afternoon sun less than half a mile from the First Cliff.

Climbing the light so that she might have a better vantage point, the terrified girl, alone with her sister at Cedar Point, observed that the British were launching boat after boat into the sea. The town was to be burned, she thought, just as the City of Washington had been destroyed.

In the village there was confusion and uproar when the boy arrived with the news. Forgetting the lighthouse, the villagers and soldiers planned to defend the shore near the town against the invaders, using the fish houses for a fort.

Then began the approach. Five large whale boats, loaded with marines and manned by British sailors, started for the beach. It was a splendid but fearful sight, the marines with their bright red coats and their guns held upright, bayonets glistening in the sun. The oars in the whaleboat moved with orderly precision as the Britishers neared the point of land where the girls were watching.

All at once Rebecca remembered that in the lighthouse residence, attached to the tower itself, were a drum and fife that belonged to the missing guardsmen who had amused themselves during their leisure by teaching the girls to play. Rebecca flew down the steps of the tower, handed her sister the drum and picked up the fife. The girls stole out of the building and hid behind the lighthouse. Then, as the steady, measured strokes of the British sailors could be heard nearing the spit of land where the lighthouse stands, Rebecca began to play the fife and her sister to beat the drum. Louder and louder came their efforts, until the British oarsmen passing the lighthouse stopped their labors. Could the Americans be massing to overcome them?

The officers in the whaleboats were in a quandary. As they were debating what to do, the ship's commander aboard the *La Hogue,* hearing the drum and fife, ran up a flag signifying danger and ordered a gun to be fired. This was the signal agreed upon for a return to the *La Hogue,* so the expedition was turned into a retreat. Cheers could be heard coming from the townspeople of Scituate as the girls, triumphant but exhausted from their efforts, sat down to rest. What a proud moment it must have been for the young girls when they realized that their ruse had saved the town of Scituate!

As darkness fell over the bay, a gun flash was seen from the British warship. A single shot, aimed at the lighthouse tower, described its parabola from the deck of the *La Hogue* but screamed into the water more than fifty yards short of the mark. It was merely a parting gesture, however, for the *La Hogue* then hoisted sail and was soon hull down bound northward. In a short time the townspeople reached Cedar Point, and the girls who comprised the American Army of Two were soon made to feel their importance.

More than half a century later Rebecca and Abigail both signed the statements below. Through the courtesy of Helen Ingersol Tetlow we publish Miss Abigail Bates's own statement:

> Abbie the Drummer one
> of the American Army of
> two in the War of 1812
>   Miss Abbie Bates
>   aged 81
>   Mass.

Miss Rebecca Bates made the following statement:

Born 1793   1878
    Rebecca Bates, aged 84 years, one of the American Army of two in the war of 1812 who with her sister aged 15 saved two large vessels laden with flour from being taken by the British with fife and drum.

In 1874 the *Saint Nicholas Magazine* published an article by Charles Barnard describing the incident. He claimed that Abigail had not helped in the Britishers' repulse, but gave the honor to a Miss Sarah Winsor, who, Barnard relates, was visiting Rebecca at the time. There is no controversy about Rebecca Bates's part in the story.

Regardless of which two girls were responsible for saving Scituate from the enemy during the War of 1812, it was a heroic incident at Scituate Lighthouse that summer of 1814. In the words of Lilla A. Ham:

> *Thus Rebecca and Abigail, loyal and true,*
> *Once composed the American Army of Two.*

PART THREE

Treasure

~~~~~~~~~

CHAPTER 1

Marshfield Mansion Gold

The thought of finding treasure appeals to almost every adventuresome person. For most of us who actually search for it, however, our efforts usually end in disappointment. Nevertheless, on at least some occasions the seeker is handsomely rewarded.

One of the rarest treasure stories, based in my hometown of Marshfield, involves an organ, a dream, a spinster and a chimney. This peculiar tale begins in the year 1789. Its principal character is Stuart Alton.

At the age of twenty-one Stuart was taken into a substantial banking business his father had founded, and for the next few years he prospered along with the rise of the town. Stuart married a local girl, and the couple had three children.

By 1807 Stuart had become interested in playing the harpsichord. The following year he journeyed to a nearby city, where he discovered a beautiful organ prominently displayed in a music store. This organ, built by the firm of Astor and Broadwood, had been constructed by George Astor himself, the brother of John Jacob Astor, and became a favorite of almost everyone who played it.

Stuart Alton not only fell in love with the organ but desired it for his own. He was only a fair player, but his interest in the organ made him anxious to improve his musical ability. He began visiting the nearby city and studying the organ with one of the leading players of the day.

Finally, in 1810, his teacher told him that he had improved sufficiently to allow him to go ahead and purchase an organ. Alton was a happy man when he found that an Astor and Broadwood organ was still on sale in the music store. Three weeks later his instrument arrived at his home, and night after night he would play the songs and hymns of the period. Once a month regularly he went to the city to take a music lesson, until finally his teacher declared that he had become an accomplished musician.

The War of 1812 brought family tragedy. Stuart's wife, returning by sea to town after visiting her son aboard the Frigate *Constitution,* was lost with all others aboard a small coastal packet. The shock was too great for Stuart. He closed the organ and decided never to play it again. To take his mind from his grief, his doctor recommended that Alton take up fishing. The banker would often row out a mile from shore, when the waves were not too high, to fish for hours at a time. One day two British sloops came in from the ocean and captured Stuart. Taken aboard one of the sloops as a prisoner, he was interrogated for over a week, then released near Pemaquid Point, Maine, whence he returned to his home.

The humiliation of his capture, together with the recent loss of his wife, led Stuart to decide to move away from the seashore and settle nearer the center of town. He purchased an attractive plot of land and renovated the fine old mansion on it. The house contained a remarkable fireplace almost large enough for a man to walk in upright. The left side was arranged as an oven.

Stuart was seriously considering playing the organ again, waiting only for the right time and opportunity. And so, across from the fireplace, in order that he might play by the firelight, he placed his organ.

In 1832, when Stuart Alton retired from business, he was

considered a fairly wealthy man. On November 1 he wrote to his children, asking that they humor an old man's wish and visit him during the coming holiday season.

All three children came with their own children, and for the next few days the house resounded with gaiety and laughter. Then, on the final night of their visit, Stuart had them all sit around the fire. He went over to the organ and began playing. Everyone expressed pleasure that Alton had decided to play again, and the former banker was a happy man when he bade them farewell the next morning. The family visits became annual affairs.

As for his organ, Alton decided that once more he could journey to the city and resume his lessons. He was forming an unusual plan in his mind. This time he went to another teacher, a musical expert on composition. Before long Stuart Alton began composing his own pieces. Those who passed his window in the summertime could hear the strains of the unusual organ melodies he was creating.

In 1851 Stuart suffered a bad fall and was unable to leave the house. Nevertheless, when winter came, he sent out his invitations to his family as usual and everyone came, transforming the house once more by the activity and gaiety. Again came the final night of the visit, with all Stuart Alton's descendants gathered in the living room, where the great logs were sparkling and blazing merrily.

Later, as the fire began to die away, old Stuart Alton hobbled across to his beloved organ. All eyes were upon him as he began his first selection. Soon his listeners noticed a strange undertone in the playing that made them uneasy. Then suddenly, without warning, the organ stopped.

By this time the light from the dying fire barely illuminated the bent form of the aged man, but they could see him faintly as he grasped the organ seat in an attempt to stand erect.

"Children," he began, "I've been practicing in my feeble way on a musical composition that I trust will interest you all. It was written in an attempt to place a special significance on what is to follow. At its conclusion I'm going to reveal something of extreme interest to every one of you, and I shall not repeat it."

Stuart Alton again sat down at the organ. He began playing. Indeed it was an unusual composition to which the entranced group listened, and as the old man worked his aged fingers up and down the keyboard there seemed to be a hidden message for each of them in his inspired playing.

At the height of his composition, as he played on with intense concentration, the others noticed that his face began to glow and his breathing became labored. They could see that it was harder and harder for him to continue.

Suddenly, at the very climax of his playing, the old man gasped, grabbed at his chest and then slumped down between the organ and the seat. His children and grandchildren rushed to him and carried him to a sofa. But it was too late, for even as they gathered around him they realized that he had suffered a shock and was dying.

"Come," he muttered feebly, "I *must* finish. . . ."

But Stuart Alton was dead.

Three days later his funeral was held in the same living room, and all who had known him attended. The minister spoke highly of Alton, and mentioned the two episodes in his life that had affected him so deeply. Then his final remains were buried in the village cemetery, and his family gathered at the local bank to hear the reading of his will.

Everyone present was surprised and disappointed, for the will merely mentioned the house, the organ and the chimney, and what was to be found therein. There was no mention of any substantial amount of money, except for scarcely more than $1200 at the bank, in an account that had seen heavy withdrawals during the last few years. And the bank's cashier declared that the withdrawals had always been in the form of ten- and twenty-dollar gold pieces.

Where then, Stuart Alton's heirs asked, could the money have gone? Two inspired members of the family decided to take the organ apart, but they got nothing for their pains except the task of reassembling it again. Then the chimney was discussed. It was carefully examined, almost brick by brick, but no hidden vaults or recesses were revealed. Finally the family members swallowed their disappointment and returned to their respective homes.

Several months later business reverses left one of the children temporarily short of money, and he sold his own home and moved into Stuart's spacious residence, where he stayed for the remainder of his life. In turn his son and daughter took over the house when the father died. The son passed away in 1896, leaving the girl, Lucy Alton, alone in the great mansion. She had become a schoolteacher, and a good one, but her pupils wondered why she lived in the great house all alone except for two cats.

Strangely enough, Lucy Alton was not in the least lonely, for the woman was fascinated by the ancient mansion. Her father had often told her of the unusual episode of her grandfather's death, and how he had been playing the organ when he died.

From the time she was a child, the organ and the fireplace had always seemed to cast a spell over her, and at an early age she learned to play the instrument. As the years went by she studied her grandfather's career, having preserved all of his letters and musical compositions that she could find. Eventually she was able to play all his compositions, especially the weird piece with the unusual ending.

When Lucy Alton retired from teaching she concentrated on the disappearance of her grandfather's wealth but came to no definite conclusion concerning it. Not one of the letters gave her the slightest clue as to the whereabouts of all those gold pieces he had taken from the bank.

Lucy Alton was the very last of the Alton line, for the War Between the States and the Spanish–American War had wiped out the remaining male members of the family. By the time of her amazing dream, which is here related, not a single relative remained alive.

One Sunday evening, as was her custom, she opened the organ. Before her she placed her grandfather's famous composition, which she played slowly and with great feeling.

At the end of the work she closed the organ, put out her cats and retired upstairs to bed. The lingering strains of the music were uppermost in her mind as she fell asleep.

In her dream a vision appeared. It was her grandfather, whom she had never seen, seated at the organ and playing the very piece she had completed a short time before. She felt herself urging him to continue his playing, to finish his composition. And that was just what the vision did. He played his musical effort through to the end, stood up and walked over to the huge fireplace. Picking up a poker, he entered the fireplace, walking to the left side, where he tapped significantly against the bricks at the back.

Then the dream faded, and Lucy sat upright in bed. Could there possibly be some unusual significance to the dream? She lay back and pulled the covers over her shivering form. Just as she was about to forget the whole episode, she heard a sound that made the blood surge violently through her veins.

Downstairs someone seemed to be actually playing the organ. Terrified, but filled with a determination to find out if someone was really at the organ, Lucy threw on her wrapper and went to the top of the stairs. The playing had stopped.

Crawling back into bed, she made a solemn resolve that she would investigate the chimney the very next morning.

Awakening early, she dressed hurriedly and traveled to the

home of the handyman of the neighborhood. After binding him to secrecy, she asked him to accompany her back to the house, and the two went into the chimney.

There Lucy told the handyman, whose name was Jim, just what her dream was about. Jim smiled tolerantly, thought to himself about the peculiarities of spinsters in general, and agreed to carry out her wish: to break through the back wall of the chimney.

He became much more interested when he noticed something that no one had ever apparently seen before. A certain brick, shoulder high, appeared to have been reinforced at one time, as if it had been removed and then cemented back into place. For tools he had only several long, thin screwdrivers and a hammer, but he had the brick loose in a little more than an hour.

Pulling it out, he examined it carefully. The brick showed evidence of mortar applied at two different periods. Then Jim flashed a light through the hole where the brick had been. There was a small area, less than three inches across, between the row of visible bricks and another row of bricks immediately in back.

Lucy was an excited observer as Jim removed the brick and found the space between the two brick walls. But she was not going to get her hopes up too high.

"What do you find in the hole?" she asked Jim.

"It's too small to see anything. Shall I take out some more bricks?"

"Of course, let's settle this once and for all."

By noon only three tiers of bricks had been removed from the chimney wall, but they were too excited to stop for lunch. At one-thirty in the afternoon Jim had made a hole large enough to reach down as far as a foot above the ground.

"Go ahead, Jim," urged Lucy, "try to find something, anything. I am getting very nervous in spite of myself."

So Jim stood up, rested a moment and then rolled his sleeve above the elbow. Thrusting his long, bare arm inside the wall, he groped lower and lower. Then there was a faint tinkle as Jim's arm started to withdraw.

"Darn it!" he cried. "I dropped it."

"Dropped what?" shouted Lucy.

"I'm not sure," he admitted, "but it felt like money!"

"For heaven's sake, try again, Jim, try again!"

This time Jim decided to pick up just one piece instead of a handful, and thrust his arm in again. His second try was successful, and the two excited people stared, fascinated, at the twenty-dollar gold piece he held up.

"Jim, we've found the treasure!"

"I guess you're right, Miss Lucy, I guess you're right."

At three o'clock that same afternoon two bank representatives were gazing in wonderment at the golden pile of ten- and twenty-dollar gold pieces that threatened to overflow the living room table where they had been placed. That night the money was counted, put in canvas bags and stored in the local bank. Lucy Alton, even after paying Jim $1000 for his efforts, was $36,600 richer than she had been the day before. And as she was the sole remaining survivor of the Altons, every cent was hers.

It seems that Stuart Alton had used the chimney as a receptacle for the gold pieces just as we use razor blade receptacles today. And that was the surprise he had planned for his family on the night of his death. No one had been clever enough to notice the brick that showed evidences of having been removed —no one except handyman Jim.

As for the dream, Lucy claimed that it happened just as she said it did. However, she did offer a reasonable explanation for the organ playing after her first dream. She believed she fell asleep after sitting up in bed and dreamed a second dream, in which she heard the playing again. In any case, she was grateful for the second dream, for otherwise, she always contended, she would never have attached any particular significance to the first.

CHAPTER 2

The Code to the Treasure

My first knowledge that there ever was a King of Calf Island came from a man whose name was King—Joe King. He conducted a business on Commercial Wharf, Boston, and I learned about him while I was collecting information concerning Apple Island, Boston harbor. I had been told that Mr. King lived for several years at Apple Island, where he often searched for the treasure supposed to have been buried there a century before.

In 1934 I interviewed him on Commercial Wharf about the Apple Island treasure, but he never acknowledged having found any money. However, before the interview ended, he had told me about certain mysterious events that had taken place in Boston's outer bay, several miles from Apple Island, where he had lived for a few summers.

Mr. King told me that out on the Brewster Islands a man known as the King of Calf Island was said to have buried something of importance, either in the foundation of a fisherman's house or in the ruins of another building. He was not sure, but it may have been pirate treasure or a clue that might lead to treasure of some sort. The story fascinated me, of course, and I determined to find out more about it as soon as possible.

The following year I decided to put into book form the information I was collecting about all the islands and lighthouses in Boston harbor. While gathering information and stories about the outer bay, I landed by canoe with Mrs. Snow at

Great Brewster Island. This high, drumlin-type island, with two hills and a flat valley between, is surrounded in large part by a government-built seawall.

The higher of the two hills, at the northern end of the island, is 104 feet, with steep cliffs on its eastern, northern and western sides; on the south it slopes gently toward the flat, level area in the middle of the island. The other hill is smaller, with cliffs on the southern and eastern sides.

From the southern tip of the island stretches an unusual bar that winds in a mighty S-shaped curve for almost two miles, ending at a channel called the Narrows, just across from Fort Warren. At the extreme tip of the bar, which is known as the Brewster Spit, there stood a lighthouse from 1856 until June 7, 1929, when it burned down. The lighthouse, called the Narrows Light, was known locally as Bug Light because of the seven spindly iron legs on which it stood. Today the spindly legs remain, but the burned lighthouse was replaced by an automatic beacon, and now no lighthouse keeper lives there.

At low tide it used to be possible to walk along Great Brewster Spit from Great Brewster to Bug Light and back in plenty of time to avoid getting your feet wet. Dredging by man has eliminated this delightful activity. Another bar goes out to Boston Light, half a mile southeast of Great Brewster. And a submerged bar, bare only once or twice a year, runs out from the northern tip of Great Brewster over to Middle Brewster Island. Usually at low water it is knee to waist deep. The bar is covered with barnacled rocks and heavy streamers of rockweed and seaweed.

After landing on the beach at Great Brewster, Mrs. Snow and I pulled the canoe high above the reach of the incoming tide. Then we hiked up the slope of the larger hill, where in a little cluster of houses we noticed smoke coming from one of the chimneys. It was here that we first met the island caretaker,

John J. Nuskey. He greeted us cordially, and soon we had learned his history.

Caretaker Nuskey was then fifty-nine years of age, a lobster fisherman by trade. He received $10 a month from the government to watch over the island where he lived. Having lost the lower part of his right leg many years before, he was known around the island as "Peg-Leg Nuskey," and walked around the island with the aid of a cane.

Pulling out notebook and pencil, I commenced my questions about the mysterious doings mentioned by Joe King. Nuskey fortified himself by taking a sizable chaw of tobacco from his pocket and then was ready for me.

"Mr. Nuskey," I began, "have you ever heard of any unusual or mysterious happenings on this island which might be of interest for the book I'm writing?"

John Nuskey thought carefully for almost a full minute, chewing away at the tobacco he had crammed into his square jaws, as if debating how much he should tell us and how much he had better refrain from mentioning. Then we could see him make up his mind. Spitting a copious amount of tobacco juice, Nuskey cleared his throat. "Well, Mr. Snow, it's a sort of yes-and-no story. I promised some years back I wouldn't tell too much of it, but it's been so long, and nothing has ever been done, that you might as well have most of the story now.

"Back in the second year I came here, 1926, there was something unusual. I've been a fisherman around here all my life almost, and got this job in 1925, but I never saw, either before or since, a man with steel rods sinking 'em all over the island, wherever he thought there might have been a house.

"This fellow, named Redwell or something like that, came down here from Canada. He had permission and everything, that part was in order, but he spent two whole weeks sinking those long, thin rods down through the ground around old cellar holes and buildings. Before he finished we were all pretty curious about it.

"Finally, I guess his vacation time was up, and he got one of us to take him into Boston. I went with him, and in the boat he wrote out something which he gave me concerning what he was doing. I have it around somewhere. The poor fellow had come all the way from Canada for nothing, I guess. Perhaps one day I'll find the paper, but I haven't seen it for years."

I questioned him further, but he was rather vague about certain points I brought up. He did promise to ask his fishing mate, whose name, for reasons obvious later, I shall refrain from mentioning.

I subsequently found out that the Government had taken over the island in 1898, when the Army planned to erect fortifications here. They abandoned their plans, and it was not until World War II that the plans were carried out.

Meanwhile, as we saw during our visit in 1935, a dozen or so families had built summer cottages on the island, paying the Government a nominal fee for this privilege. Among the families then on the island was that of Mrs. Gertrude Crowley, who lived here with her two children. Later I learned that Mrs. Crowley's grandfather was James Turner, otherwise known as the King of Calf Island, the man for whom I searched.

For the next few years we made summertime calls in our canoe at Great Brewster Island, and John Nuskey was always a pleasant host. We would pull our canoe above the tide, make a little fire and enjoy a meal. Usually before the meal ended Caretaker Nuskey, supporting himself with his cane, would come limping down the hill to greet us, his peg leg making cuplike depressions in the sand.

He pointed out many things, including the deep Worthylake well, located halfway up the big hill and dug some time before 1695 by the father of the first keeper of Boston Light. We would often climb the hill to drink the water there. And, as it happened, it was the last place we ever saw John Nuskey alive.

Then came the month of September 1940. I was teaching school in Winthrop at the time, and my wife and I always tried to plan a long canoe trip just before the beginning of my educational duties. On September 5, an hour before sunrise, we were down on the Winthrop shore with our notebooks, food and cameras. I carried the canoe to the water's edge and loaded it. Soon we were paddling away for our last day of adventure before the start of school.

Sunrise caught us as we rounded George's Island. After visiting several other locations, we reached Great Brewster Spit, at Bug Light. We took a swim and then paddled along on the northern side of the spit, finally arriving at a formidable ledge known as the Black Rocks, located close by the spit. Paddling toward the ledge, we decided to get out there and rest our weary limbs, for we had already covered a considerable distance. I steadied the canoe while Anna-Myrle stepped out across the bow onto the barnacle-covered ledge. Then she stood up, her white bathing suit glistening in the morning sun.

Suddenly, without the slightest warning, there was a cry from the other side of the rocks.

"Say, what are you?" came an astonished voice. "Are you one of those things called mermaids?"

The voice was that of John Nuskey, who was in his lobster boat hauling traps in the deep water on the other side of the ledge. As he explained later, he had seen Anna-Myrle's head and shoulders appear above the rocks. Wearing the white bathing suit, she must have presented quite a picture to Nuskey, who up to that moment had seen neither the canoe nor its occupants, for our approach had been shielded by the Black Rocks. We had not seen Nuskey either, until startled by his amazed shout when he noticed Anna-Myrle's form as it appeared to rise out of the sea.

My wife and I returned to the canoe, paddled around the Black Rocks and brought the canoe up to the lobster boat, holding onto the gunwale with our hands.

"Say," Nuskey began, "it's strange that I should have seen you appear that way just now, for I've been looking out for you for two weeks. When you get a chance, come over to the island and meet me up by the well. I'll be finished hauling soon. I've got something to show you."

We agreed that after we visited Graves Light and Boston Light we would return to Great Brewster Island for a rest and some food.

It was shortly after two o'clock that our canoe grounded on the shale at Great Brewster. We had made our circuit of the harbor and were very tired and hungry. I pulled the craft up above the reach of the tide, and Anna-Myrle began preparations for cooking bacon and eggs for our late lunch. But I had been wondering what Nuskey was going to show me, and soon clambered up the bank and reached the well. He was there waiting for me, smiling broadly.

"I've been watching you for the past hour," he admitted. "Boy, you must be tired. You know, I'd never trust myself in one of those canoes. They look too dangerous." We both took a deep drink of water from the Worthylake well, and then he turned to me.

"That gave me quite a start this morning, when your wife appeared that way. It sort of made me wonder whether I shouldn't tell you the whole story." He paused, then went on. "Well, in the first place, I found the paper. The man's name wasn't Redwell, as I said, but Tom Redwick, and here it is on the paper." Nuskey handed me a grimy piece of yellow paper, on which the following statement was written:

Write Thomas Redwick, General Delivery Kingston, Ontario, if you find old book on Brewster Island, cover of skin, message inside. In old sail in foundation fisherman home. Good reward I promise.

Thomas Redwick

John Nuskey went on with his explanation. "Of course Redwick was the Canadian stranger, and I found out later that his grandfather was a relative of Captain Turner, the old Bug Light keeper who became King of Calf Island. I found the paper a couple of weeks ago." Nuskey took another deep drink of water, then continued with his story.

"My fishing mate and I always wondered what it could be. We were never going to tell anyone, but we're not getting along too well lately, for he seems to be getting ugly, dang him. Perhaps you'll be able to figure out something that we couldn't. Go to it."

Excited beyond belief at the actual evidence of a message that told of something buried in the outer harbor, I examined the paper carefully. Then the words Brewster Island caught my eye. There were four Brewster Islands, and why not look on one of the others? Boston Light at Little Brewster would be too small and open to attempt any hiding there, while Outer Brewster was separated by a deep channel from Middle Brewster, connected by bar to Great Brewster. Yes, as I suggested to John Nuskey, it was perhaps likely that Middle Brewster was the island to visit. He seemed to agree with the possibility.

An hour later, after a delicious lunch, my wife and I climbed the bank together. This time I had my camera, and we found Nuskey down by the well again. We talked for perhaps ten minutes.

"You know," he said, "I've been thinking over what you

said. I may go over to Middle Brewster and look around myself." Shortly afterward I asked him to stand down near the well, and I took several pictures of him there. Those photographs were the last ever taken of Caretaker Nuskey.

On September 9, 1940, an overturned skiff floated ashore on the jagged rocks of Middle Brewster Island. It belonged to Caretaker Nuskey, but there was no sign of the sixty-four-year-old fisherman, who had then been missing since the afternoon of September 5. His cane, without which he could not walk, was lying near his house on Great Brewster.

At three o'clock in the afternoon of Monday, September 16, Patrolman James A. Melvin of the Hull Police Department was notified by a resident of the vicinity that there was a body on Nantasket Beach, some three hundred yards north of where the old schooner *Nancy* had come ashore in 1927. Patrolman Melvin went to the scene, where he found the lifeless remains of Peg-Leg Nuskey.

Later, when Mrs. Snow and I read of the strange death of our friend, it gave us a weird sensation, for we realized that we might have been the last ones to see him alive. John Nuskey, had he desired to reach Middle Brewster Island, could not have hiked across because of his peg leg, but would have rowed over in his skiff. It was entirely possible that he had journeyed across to Middle Brewster that very afternoon of our visit, and there met his death in a manner we shall never know. He may well have died in pursuit of the treasure of Captain Turner, keeper of Bug Light and King of Calf Island.

I recalled an interview I had conducted some years before on Deer Island, Boston harbor, with Wesley Pingree, former keeper of Deer Island Light. His father, Henry Pingree, was erstwhile keeper of Boston Light. I went through my papers and found the record of our conversation, which follows:

"If you want a colorful figure for the outer bay, it was Captain Turner, without question. A giant in size, he had a long, flowing beard. He fled down here from the Great Lakes around 1845 and settled on Calf Island. When the Government finished Bug Light in 1856, James Turner was given the position as keeper. He remained there over thirty years.

"I'll never forget when I first heard about Captain Turner. I was just a lad at the time, and probably a little fresh. I wanted to hike across the bars from Boston Light down to Bug Light and visit him. Then, when I got there, I stayed too long, and he realized he'd have to row or sail me back home, for the spit was covered with water.

"He sailed back to Boston Light with me, but before doing so he went over to Fort Warren for the mail. I made such a fuss at his not taking me right back to Boston Light that he decided to teach me a lesson. Just off the Boston Light wharf he reached over, grabbed me by the scruff of the neck and, before I realized what was happening, tossed me into the sea. He knew I could swim, all right, but he never turned around once to see if I got ashore alive! He sailed away to Bug Light, probably rather pleased with himself for teaching me a lesson.

"Father watched me as I crawled up on shore like a wet kitten. Although he was smiling, he warned me to be careful in the future. He told me that I'd had it coming, probably, but that I should be cautious of what I did in the future in the presence of Captain Turner. He explained that Captain Turner had lost his temper once on the Great Lakes, killing a man with a barrel stave there. Rest assured, I never bothered Turner again. They always said he was a pirate, and had brought treasure with him when he landed in Massachusetts. He came to Chatham first, they say, for he was afraid the Boston police were looking for him. But we really never knew."

Two other clues helped me to build a better picture of the King of Calf Island. Landing at Calf Island one day, I met an old man, Mr. Augustus Reekast, who dated everything from the Chelsea Fire of 1908.

He told me he had something to show me—pictures of the island the way it formerly was—and the next time I met him he gave me a folded magazine story to read about the outer harbor islands, an article that included a picture labeled "The King of Calf Island." I had never expected to see a sketch of Captain Turner, and was tremendously pleased.

The article was written by William H. Rideing and had been published in *Harper's* in August 1884. Evidently Mr. Rideing found Turner just as interesting as I later discovered him to be:

> The occupants of the other islands are lobster-men, chief among them being old Turner, who from time immemorial has hauled his pots in the waters surrounding the Brewsters. . . . I do not imagine that old Turner ever smiles; his deep-lined visage is puckered with seriousness, and though he is not talkative, an unexplained pathos speaks out from his eyes, which are screened from the forehead by a bristling pair of brows. He has been so saturated with salt water for nearly fourscore years that he has a half-pickled appearance, and his beard and the curly locks which still flourish, though bleached by age and exposure, are always wet with brine.

The second clue I uncovered at the Hull Town Hall, where an examination of the vital statistics showed that Captain James John Turner was born February 12, 1803, and died in Hull on March 12, 1888, at the age of eighty-five years and one month. Although the details concerning his father were missing, Turner came from Brighton, England, where his mother's maiden name had been Hannah Cronan. Captain Turner was buried at Mount Auburn Cemetery in Cambridge, Massachusetts.

I also discovered that either Turner or a friend had cut the date of his birthday on a Calf Island ledge, back in 1851. Later I found out that Turner enjoyed hiking around the outer harbor islands, as he was often seen by the keeper of Boston Light, his huge form moving rapidly along the low-tide gravel bars of the outer bay.

Night after night I worried over a nautical chart, wondering if Turner could have hiked across to Middle Brewster. I thought that it was at best an outside chance. On the other hand, the message did not specify which Brewster Island was meant.

World War II intervened and I went overseas, returning later as a casualty. After I had reached home, I was going through my belongings in the attic one day when I came across the chart over which I had pondered so often.

At the end of the war I made up a party and went out to Great Brewster Island with Captain William Van Leer, aboard his vessel the *Charlesbank.* When I suggested a hike across to Middle Brewster, only a few others besides Mrs. Snow decided to make the venture.

It was not an easy day to make our crossing. To begin with, there was neither a new-moon tide nor a full-moon tide, both of which bring unusually low water. In addition, the waves that day were rather rough. But an hour before low water we started across in pairs to support each other and prevent slipping, and soon were more than halfway across. From then on it was deeper water and we were up to our waists, sliding and scraping along over the barnacle-covered rocks and through the heavy kelp and rockweed. No one who has made that crossing ever forgets it. Time after time the boisterous waves battered us off our feet. When we arrived at Middle Brewster Island, our ankles and legs were cut and bleeding from scores of encounters with barnacles.

The others decided to hike around the outer circumference of the island and explore the cliffs and semicaves there. But my objective was the cliffs toward the center of the island, where the Richard S. Whitney property was located.

The Whitney's residence proved to be the only building old enough to have been visited over a century before by Captain Turner. When I had phoned Mrs. Whitney to get permission for my trip, she had said that the building was purchased from an old fisherman on the island and that her husband had rebuilt the house, modernizing it at the time. Then he had erected a giant flagpole on the ledge above the house. I asked Mrs. Whitney about the cellar, and she said that although in the middle of the living room there was a trapdoor that led down into the cellar, they had rarely opened it, and not one of the family had ever examined the basement. Of course, there was no known reason for their going down into the cellar.

I went up to the Whitney house and surveyed the ruins. The giant flagpole had fallen across the backwall at the top of the island. I read the inscription on it: ERECTED BY RICHARD S. WHITNEY 1902. Down below, the ruins of the Whitney home stood, the western ell smashed in, every window missing, the roof stripped of shingles. The years had taken their inevitable toll with a vengeance.

Gingerly I made my way across the kitchen floor to the living room, where the three-foot-square trapdoor awaited me. Surrounded by the ruins of what had once been exquisite furniture, the wooden square proved a formidable barrier to my plan of entering the cellar. After fifteen minutes of pounding and prying, I forced a corner up, and the rest was easy.

A pit of blackness awaited below, smelling musty and unused. I lowered myself into the pit, and as soon as my eyes were accustomed to the darkness, I began exploring the area. Then a rat, disturbed from its nest, scampered across my body, and I was not too anxious to keep on with my explorations. After resting a moment to recover my nerve, I continued. It must have been another half hour before I came across what appeared to be a collection of old rags, piled up in a heap in the southeastern corner of the cellar. I kicked at them, and seemed to hit something fairly solid. Could it be another rat? I kicked again, rather cautiously, for in my bathing trunks and sneakers I could not offer much opposition to an outraged rodent.

At my second kick the mass went to pieces, leaving a dismembered book, which I gazed at in complete astonishment. My last kick had broken the binding of the volume, separating it into two sections.

What a disappointment! Merely an old book, I thought, discarded years ago by the fisherman, not important enough to take away with him. But wait, could it possibly be that unknown object for which so many had looked? Could that book contain a secret treasure map or document?

Picking up the two sections of the volume I had kicked apart, I wrapped the pages in several rags, which actually were crumbling folds of canvas. Climbing up through the trapdoor, I replaced the wooden square in the floor and made my way down to where the others were waiting. They saw the canvas-wrapped bundle.

"What do you have there?" they asked.

"Oh, just an old book I found in a cellar," I replied.

No one appeared to show unusual interest. Unfortunately for our plans, I had taken too long down in the cellar, for the tide had gone out and was then almost two hours in. We all made our way down over the rocks to the tidal bar, joined hands again for safety and started back. In several places the tide was neck deep and I held the canvas-wrapped book high in the air. When we gained the shallow water at Great Brewster Island, the volume was still untouched by the sea.

That night I carefully examined what I had found in the old cellar. It was a volume 7 by 9 1/2 inches in size, 1 1/4 inches thick. The outer covering was of skin, said by some to be human. Inside the cardboard-reinforced cover was a statement pasted against the heavy paper. It was signed by one of the consuls on the island of Malta:

Malta/20 November 1839
I hereby certify that to my personal knowledge this volume belonged to the library of the Knights of St. John of Malta of the order of Jerusalem.
Witness my hand on this day and year above written——

Robt Ligetz

On the front flyleaf was written a single word, *Vertiz.* On the title page of the volume was the following, written in Italian:

L'AMBASCIADORE POLITICO CRISTIAN OPERA
DI
CARLO MARIA CARAFA
PRINCIPE DI BVTERA, & C.

Written by hand on the outer skin of the volume, evidently by a scribe in the Malta library, was the following title and numbers:

POLITICO CRISTIANO
352

The volume was printed August 1, 1690, on a private printing press in Mazzarini, Sicily, and was extremely rare. No other known copy in North America was as old as mine. Bookworms and rats had eaten into almost half the more than two hundred pages. All through the volume various pages had been corrected by pen.

After examining the volume from cover to cover, I discovered a secret compartment between the recesses of a double page, but there was nothing inside, much to my disappointment.

Later I telephoned Mrs. Whitney and told her about the book, but she said that never had either she or her husband owned such a volume, and by the laws of treasure-trove the book was mine to keep.

I showed the volume to several friends.* One of them, Robert M. Evans, who read Italian readily, pronounced it rather uninteresting except for those portions especially concerned with procedure in the papal courts.

Later I took the volume to the Rare Book Department of the Boston Public Library, where I showed it to my friend, Miss Harriet Swift. She had often helped me while I was gathering material for my first book, published in 1935, and I knew that she would be interested in what I had discovered.

Returning a week later, I found that she had identified the book as a rare one. But when I mentioned my hope that there might be a clue regarding buried treasure, she smiled tolerantly.

However, a few days later my telephone rang. It was Miss Swift, and from her manner she was a little excited. "Come in here just as soon as you can, Mr. Snow, for I've something to show you."

An hour later I was in the Rare Book Department, where Miss Swift greeted me.

"I know that it's foolish to get excited, but I may have

---

*In 1971 the author and his wife were bound and gagged in their home while the Italian book and other items were stolen. None of the items was ever recovered.

something for you," she said as she opened my old book at pages 100 and 101. "Look carefully," she went on, trying to conceal her excitement.

I glanced carefully at the open volume but saw nothing unusual.

"Hold up page 101 so that the light shines through," she suggested.

I did so, and except for a few words that had been rewritten, there was nothing to notice. There were about 270 words printed in Italian, but nothing of importance, or so it seemed to me. Concealing my disappointment, for I had come all the way from Winthrop evidently for nothing, I continued to study page 101.

"Well," said Miss Swift, "what can you tell me?"

"Except for a few smudges and a little rewriting of the letters, there's nothing unusual," was my answer.

"Nothing unusual?" Miss Swift smiled. "That page actually contains a crude attempt at a coded message. Study it and you may have your answer as to why the book was hidden. For example, glance at the eleventh line up from the bottom of the page."

I did so, and found that the line had been corrected in pen, probably centuries ago. I studied it carefully, trying to read it aloud in my best Italian pronunciation. *"Appostolica. Sceso di poi l'Ambasciadore dal palchetto."*

"Never mind what it says," Miss Swift broke in. "The line itself isn't important. I was first drawn to it by the unusual corrections in ink. You see, *Sceso di poi* was evidently written in as a correction by the printer or proofreader after the volume was finished and bound. That of course is interesting, but not as important as the next word. Look carefully at the next word, *l'Ambasciadore.* Do you see anything unusual about the *o* and the *r*?"

Suddenly I realized what she meant. Over each of the two letters was a small hole or pinprick in the page itself. Miss Swift had discovered the secret of the book, and there was probably a hidden message pinpricked into the paper of page 101, each tiny hole placed exactly over a certain letter. There were about forty-five pinpricks.

Whoever had done the work had not been careful, for the holes had gone through the back of the paper and through the next page. But as page 101 was the only page where the holes hit exactly over letters, we knew that neither on page 102, 103 or 104 could there be a message.

"Now go home and see what you can discover, young man," Miss Swift suggested.

Gratefully acknowledging my thanks, I returned home and stayed up half the night trying to arrange the pinpricks so that they meant something.

After arranging and rearranging the words that contained pinpricks on them, I worked out a system that eventually allowed me to solve the code.

For the benefit of those who prefer to forgo the work of translating essentially what is on page 101, Robert M. Evans translated it as follows: "Page 101 consists of a series of rather involved directions covering the somewhat stilted protocol to be observed at the Papal Court upon the occasion of an Ambassador to His Holiness presenting his credentials and delivering to his Secretary of State the message entrusted to him by the King who sent him."

Thus I came to feel that there was nothing of importance in the translation of the pages that had the pinpricks, and that any possible solution lay in the arrangement of the pinpricked letters or words. For the purpose of simplification, from the approximately 270 words on page 101 in the Italian volume, I list below only those necessary for the eventual solution, the words that were overscored with pinpricks, with small black dots for identification:

br̊evemente	Ambasciȧta	ḃaciata	r̊ispondera
brėvita	nůȯva	cerem̊onie	ȧpparacchiaṫo
sȧlutera	chinando	occ̊orrera	dovrȧnno
ȧmbi	genuiḷettre	osṡequio	parimente
g̊enuflessione	Saṅtita	l'Ambasciadȯr̊e	ṫornera
ṡi	Maeṡtro	cėrem̊onie	Ambasciador̊e
ṫra	Nipoṫe	ṡegretario	stȧto
sė	eccėdere	nůmero	andare
genuflesṡione	deḷ	sȯg̊lio	

Actually, the secret code was not really a code at all, merely the simplest form of deception, a form Edgar Allan Poe or A. Conan Doyle probably would have scorned, so simple that it may fool the average reader even now. So in all fairness I suggest that you do not read ahead for the solution until you have made at least a slight effort to solve the puzzle yourself; you already possess every clue necessary to solve the message.

The solution of the message that led to finding the treasure at Cape Cod follows:

Placing the pinpricked letters of each line side by side we get the following result:

> RABR
> ETUOMAHT
> AHCDN
> ALSI
> GNORT

SSEER
TTSA
EEUD
SIDLOG

An effort to solve the message by putting down the first letter in each line gets the reader nowhere. Another possibility is to arrange all the characters side by side, as follows: RA-BRETUOMAHTAHCDNALSIGNORTSSEERTTSAEEUDSIDLOG
The solution still eludes us. Even by alternating the letters, first taking every other letter and every other third letter, the results are neither satisfying nor instructive.

Finally, after many hours of experimentation, you may try writing the letters backwards: GOLDISDUEEASTTREESSTRONG-ISLANDCHATHAMOUTERBAR
Introducing the spaces at the proper intervals, you can read:

GOLD IS DUE EAST TREES STRONG ISLAND
CHATHAM OUTER BAR

The next step after finding the directions on page 101 of the Italian book was to act on the information. The discovery of the book and its code had been announced in the local papers, and Mrs. Gertrude Crowley of Winthrop, granddaughter of the bearded Captain Turner of Calf Island and Bug Light fame, volunteered the information that her family had always heard Captain Turner had buried not one but two boxes of treasure, both down on Cape Cod, before he ever came to Boston Harbor.

It seemed to me that the best method of looking for the treasure was by metal detector. I sent for one from Palo Alto, California. We tested it and it appeared to be satisfactory, reacting to metal from four to five feet down.

The following week I reached Chatham and went to work,

lining up the old trees on Strong Island with the outer bar due east. It was very disappointing. Every fragment of old ship-wreck or ship timber in the vicinity had its own metal spikes or strapping of iron, and the chains and metal of various sorts in the vicinity made the hunt harder and harder.

My visits continued day after day, weekend after weekend. Although I found an amazing amount of almost every sort of iron or brass and copper fragments, there was nothing resem-bling gold.

One night I went to see Good Walter Eldridge, and after that he rowed over to visit me from time to time. His eyes would glisten with excitement as he watched me work. He would not offer to help but would always be encouraging. And when he went away he would say: "Well, I've got to go out to *my* treasure ship soon, and see if she's coming out of the sand down there on the bottom." But when Good Walter would return and I'd ask him about it, he'd say, "No, I haven't gone out yet."

October came, and with it the last Cape Cod summer visitors vanished, the people Captain Nickerson calls the "health eat-ers."

It was a Friday afternoon when the metal detector paid for its cost. I had already hit six "duds" that morning, and after lining up Chatham Light radio mast with a point of land nearby for my bearings, I set out again, slowly and painstakingly walk-ing between the long wooden handles of the detector. My ear-phones on, I watched the M-Scope indicator as the needle rose and fell.

The sun was still hot and strong, and I was just about to stop and take a drink of water when the needle gave a little jump. The hum of the phones increased correspondingly. It did not seem too important at the time, for on several other occasions the recording had actually been much higher.

I recrossed the area from side to side, and the phones

hummed encouragingly at each crossing. Finally I had centered the area of activity to a spot a yard in diameter, and it was there that I prepared to dig. Setting down the indicator, I returned to the boat for my spade, and was soon hard at work.

Throwing up spadeful after spadeful of sand, I dug until I was two feet below the surface. The sand kept sliding back in, and so I widened the pit I was making. Soon my waist was almost even with the top of the pit, but I had found nothing. Whatever metal had caused the M-Scope reaction was still undiscovered.

Resting briefly, I wiped the perspiration from my brow. Eventually I was ready for another try, but I needed a little reassurance that the metal was still there. Surely enough, when I tried out the M-Scope, the needle rose higher than ever.

Still, it would do that if I were getting closer to any object, be it iron, brass, copper, pieces of eight or doubloons. Finally I was down so far that I knew I would have to strike something soon. Measuring from the surface, I had almost reached the downward limits of the detector's power. Desperately I plunged the spade into the center of the pit—and struck a hard object six inches down. It felt like wood, but it seemed to yield.

I dropped to my knees and scraped feverishly at the sand with my bare hands, until I reached what my spade had encountered: a piece of rotten wood. Tossing it aside, I came across another and still another fragment of decayed wood. Then there was an entire area spotted with minute, rotted fragments of some type of wooden container.

Grabbing the spade again, I dug in four or five times and then threw the combined mass of sand and rotted wood out of the pit. Holding the spade for another plunge, I pressed it firmly with my left foot, but the spade went down just a few inches, clinking to a stop against a hard, metallic-like object that did not yield to pressure.

Could it be the object for which I searched, or was it merely another spike attached to an ancient, forgotten shipwreck?

There was only one way of finding out, and again I dropped to my knees and began pawing away the sand, digging and scraping until my fingers were almost bleeding. Then my finger-nails clawed across the top of a small chest.

At the possibility of actually finding treasure, I fought a losing battle with myself—a vain struggle to keep nerves and blood pressure at normal level. I was excited and tense despite all my efforts to be calm.

Impatiently scattering the broken bits of wood out of the way, my probing fingers were soon surrounding the upper section of the box, which was about eight inches wide and six inches square. Tugging and pulling, I finally released it from the sand that had held it for over a century. The lid would not open, so I pried it up with the spade point.

I was not disappointed. There, revealed to my fascinated, unbelieving eyes, was a collection of silver and gold coins, covered with rust, sand and ancient bits of paper. I sank exhausted against the side of the pit.

I had reached my objective! *I had found treasure!*

Two days later, when the excitement had died down a trifle, an appraisal of my collection was attempted. The most costly piece of all, strangely enough, was not a Spanish doubloon nor a Portuguese moidore, but an old silver piece of eight, misshapen and apparently of low value. Robert I. Nesmith, famed collector and writer on Spanish and South American coins, gave me a surprisingly large amount for the piece of eight, which he identified as one of unusual rarity. In all, the 316 coins I found in the treasure box were worth almost $1800, not a large sum by today's values, but neither a small one.

Whenever my thoughts go back to the King of Calf Island and his treasure, I still have a strange feeling about the entire affair. There are so many questions that were not answered, chief among them the following:

Why and how did Caretaker Nuskey meet his death?

Why did James Turner hide his rare volume in a Middle Brewster Island cellar?

Where did Turner get the rare volume in the first place?

Why did Turner bury the treasure so far from his home at Calf Island?

These four questions hold the key to the unsolved part of this strange mystery, but it is my belief that the answers will never be found.

Treasures of
Martha's Vineyard

There are many stories of treasure connected with the delightful island of Martha's Vineyard. Each of the tales that I have enjoyed most has an unusual distinguishing feature—a French galleon, a blue rock, a secret staircase. However, just because a story is enjoyable does not mean that it is true. Of the three mentioned above, it is probable that the French treasure tale is valid.

During the Revolution a French galleon was wrecked on the south side of the Vineyard. The ship was carrying a large sum of money, part of the payroll for the French troops then in America. Her officers, believing it impossible to transport the money to the troops, buried it with the intention of later returning and delivering it to the proper authorities. For some reason they never came back.

The money remained in its underground resting place until many years later when, according to tradition, a horseman riding along a path that followed the shore of one of the Great Ponds discovered it when his horse broke through the marsh and stuck a foot into the chest. The finder, being a man of unusual uprightness, informed the authorities of his discovery. The Federal Government took charge of the matter and claimed the money, but a substantial reward was given to the finder. In 1946, when I gave Joseph C. Allen, Martha's Vineyard historian, a helicopter ride to Gay Head Light, he told me that one of the great fortunes on the island was based on the reward given for the recovery of the money.

Then there is the story of the Blue Rock of Chappaquiddick. This enormous boulder of blue stone is located near the shore not too far from where Cape Poge Light now stands. One day at dusk a local farmer was searching for a cow when he heard the sound of oars and voices. As pirates and other people of questionable character often sailed in close to Chappaquiddick, the farmer hid in the woods and waited to see who was approaching.

A short time later a group of men landed on the beach. Pulling their craft above the water, they lifted from it a heavy chest, which they proceeded to carry to the Blue Rock. One man, who appeared to be the leader of the group, directed the others to dig a hole near the boulder. This done, they lowered the chest into the hole.

Suddenly the leader turned on the two nearest men, shot them dead and ordered their bodies thrown into the hole with the chest. The others then quickly filled the hole with dirt and hurriedly departed the island.

The farmer who had witnessed this nefarious activity decided it would be safer to wait until morning to investigate the site. But when he came back at dawn he could find no trace of either the chest or the bodies of the two murdered men. He tried to locate the buried chest time and again, always without success. To this day the story remains a mystery.

The tale of the treasure of the secret staircase is another that has never been proven. The staircase itself does actually exist. It is in the famous Daggett House, a snug little pre-Revolutionary inn on a waterfront street, where seafaring men gathered for many years. The building was the first tavern on Martha's Vineyard.

The secret staircase, which goes off from the dining room of the inn to the floor above, has a door that is so completely concealed behind a cupboard-like arrangement that the average person would never even dream of its existence.

I have talked with Marguerite Miller, manager of the Daggett House, and with Fred H. Chirgwin about this unusual set of steps. I have also walked up and down them, observing the dents in two of the stairs. According to tradition, the dents are the result of the steps being forcibly hit with heavy bags or chests of treasure as they were carried up or down the stairs.

Irrefutably the dents are there. Whether or not they were made by pirate treasure bags is a mystery never to be solved. Marguerite Miller told me of an article published by the Dukes County Historical Society, suggesting that the staircase was secreted behind the panel to enable sailors to hide from the impress gangs that were on the island. However, I believe that the steps were built to accommodate the smuggling or piratical activities of some citizen or citizens of Martha's Vineyard prone to work of that nature. Undoubtedly, a staircase concealed so carefully was constructed for a purpose that also had to be concealed, and I do not doubt that smugglers or pirates trod it at regular intervals. It is quite possible that the dents were created by a chance encounter with some of their bags or chests of loot. I do have reservations, however, about the particular pirate story connected with the secret staircase.

Late in 1846 the brig *Splendid* cleared from the port of Salem, Massachusetts. Her master, Captain Harding, was sailing with an assorted cargo around the Cape of Good Hope, bound for the East Indies. Hidden away in a large iron-bound oak chest in the captain's cabin were $60,000 packed in sixty canvas bags, each bag containing $1000 and weighing fifty-six pounds. This hoard was in addition to the substantial sum necessary to have aboard ship in those days to conduct regular commercial business in distant ports.

The silver had been brought aboard when no one was around. The captain and the mate, Howard Walker, planned to add to their combined fortunes as a result of the trip. Captain Harding had locked the chest and hidden the key in a secret compartment in the cabin, but Walker soon found out where it was by cautiously observing the master. Walker, a former pirate, had brought aboard a private collection of drugs that he planned to use to his advantage at the first opportunity.

Walker managed, without having suspicion fall on himself, to drug the captain, who died soon afterward. He then took control of the ship and the money. Eventually he arrived with his hoard on Martha's Vineyard.

It is here that the secret staircase enters the story. According to the tale, Pirate Walker concealed his treasure temporarily in the room at the top of the secret staircase in the Daggett House while making arrangements for a permanent home across on the mainland at Falmouth, Cape Cod.

It was not long before Walker decided he was ready to leave Martha's Vineyard. Obtaining the help of several local fishermen—for a good price, of course—one dark night Walker hauled his treasure down the secret staircase, out of the Daggett House and into the waiting craft. A course was set for Falmouth. By two o'clock the hustling men had anchored the vessel, gone ashore with the treasure and dug out a shallow pit near the sandy beach. Tradition tells us that when the sun rose all the money had been buried, and Captain Walker hastily placed a bright red scarf around the base of the nearest tree in order to identify the hiding place.

Walker then went into the village to conduct some business relating to the property he wished to buy. He had not been there very long when he heard from an excited merchant of a buried treasure just found near the beach. His informant told Walker that a fisherman, returning from his daily trip, had pulled his dory up on the shore and started for his home. Noticing a red scarf tied to a tree, he became curious and searched the area. He soon spotted freshly spaded earth nearby. On investigating further, he uncovered a treasure hoard. Rushing into town, he told the authorities. They commandeered a wagon and team, returned to the spot, loaded the treasure aboard and brought it to the local bank, where it was safely locked away.

Walker was in a state of shock and rage, but he could do nothing without giving himself away. It was only a matter of time, however, before investigations led to his arrest and conviction for robbery and piracy on the high seas.

That is the account of the treasure of the secret staircase. Whether or not it is true in any or all details is a question. However, I would suggest that anyone intelligent enough to steal such a sum of money in such a devilishly clever manner and manage to move it all the way from a ship at sea to Martha's Vineyard, and then conceal it in a room at the top of a secret staircase, would not be foolish enough to identify its final hiding place with a brilliant red scarf.

Two young girls, alone at Scituate Light, frightened away a British invasion force during the War of 1812 by playing a fife and drum in imitation of American troops ready to defend the shore. The girls thus earned the title "American Army of Two."

Two latter-day Jonahs, Peleg Nye of Cape Cod and James Bartley of England, were caught in the jaws of great sperm whales but lived to tell of their terrible ordeal.

Lighthouse keepers and their isolated families have delighted in the appearance of the Flying Santa since 1927. This family at Boston Light stands by their message to Santa Edward Rowe Snow and holds aloft the package of gifts just dropped.

Maritime rivalry prompted Bostonians to ensure that the *Britannia* be extricated from iced-over Boston harbor to sail as scheduled. With

great difficulty a channel was cut in the ice, and on Feb. 3, 1844, the
ship sailed off with a noisy and colorful farewell.

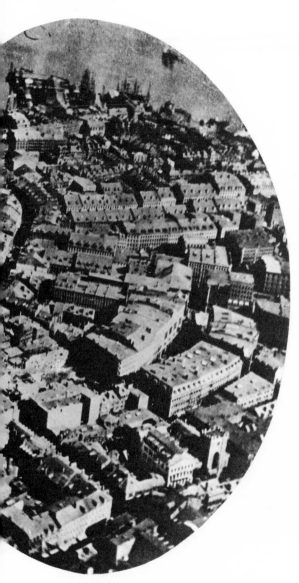

James Wallace Black took these photographs on Oct. 13, 1860, from a balloon tethered 1200 feet above Boston. This feat earned him recognition as America's first aerial photographer.

Author Edward Rowe Snow and Fred H. Chirgwin hold open the cleverly concealed door of a secret staircase in the Daggett House on Martha's Vineyard. The stairs lead to a room in which pirate Howard Walker may have stored his ill-gotten treasure. *Frederick G. S. Clow*

A battered lifeboat in a Lübeck, Germany, church memorializes the eighty-one sailors who drowned in 1957 when Hurricane Carrie capsized the training ship *Pamir*.

Following a fearful blizzard, this anchor from the *Minerva* washed ashore along with bodies and fragments of wood from the doomed ship.
Susan DiGregorio-White

Below: King, the captain's Newfoundland dog on the *Harpooner,* helped to save many passengers and crew from that foundering ship in 1816 by swimming to land with a log line through turbulent seas.

PART FOUR

Historical Anecdotes

CHAPTER 1

America's First Thanksgiving— at Clarke's Island

Few of us realize the unusual chain of events that led the Pilgrims to decide eventually on Plymouth harbor for a settlement.

The *Mayflower* arrived at Cape-End harbor, or Provincetown harbor as it is called today, on November 11, 1620. The women went ashore to do a great washing, while the men made plans to explore the area.

Many historians claim that the Pilgrims intended to settle in Virginia but changed their minds while at Provincetown harbor and decided on Massachusetts. I have always believed they had the idea of a New England settlement from the beginning, merely talking about Virginia while planning otherwise. The reason is that while New England was a wilderness, there would be neither an established Anglican Church nor an established government, both of which then existed in Virginia.

In any case, the men brought ashore at Provincetown a longboat, called a shallop, and began to repair it for a voyage of exploration. Meanwhile a party of sixteen set off hiking and exploring. They eventually returned with corn stored by the Indians, which they had found on the way.

At last the shallop was ready. Thirty-three men went aboard

under the command of Captain Jones of the *Mayflower,* who had been named chief of the expedition because of his "kindnes & forwardnes."

The shallop reached Corn Hill, where they had earlier found corn on their first hike. With the aid of cutlasses and swords, they broke through the snow and frozen ground to gather a great abundance of corn, which they brought back on the shallop to Provincetown.

The corn so pleased those on board the *Mayflower* that there were many who now suggested settling at Corn Hill. Mate Robert Coffin, however, told the others about Thievish harbor, which was more suitable than Corn Hill for a settlement.

The morning of December 6, 1620, found eighteen men aboard the shallop, intending to sail up the coast until they entered Thievish harbor and then to go ashore. Among the eighteen were ten Pilgrims who had volunteered to make the trip with the crew, including Robert Coffin, William Bradford, Myles Standish, Stephen Hopkins and John Carver, who later became the first governor of the Plymouth colony. Stephen Hopkins had taken along his servant, Edward Dotey.

It was a bitter cold day, typical of December, with a hard wind whipping across Massachusetts Bay. The spray from the waves froze on their clothes, which turned to "coates of iron." Several of the men became sick "unto death" from seasickness, while others fainted from the cold. They went ashore that night somewhere along Wellfleet Bay and discovered where Indians had been cutting up a huge black fish. While camping that night on shore, they were attacked by Indians, but fortunately they were able to fight off the intruders.

The next morning another high wind hit the coast, but the Pilgrims pushed off from shore. Soon it was snowing hard, and by midafternoon an easterly gale began lashing the area. At the mercy of wind, waves and snow, which obliterated all coastline, the Pilgrims were in desperate straits. Suddenly a great billow smashed into the shallop. The strain on the rudder proved too much, and it snapped off. The men were now unable to keep the craft before the wind, although two oars made it possible to hold a course of sorts.

They were approaching land. With darkness settling over the ocean, it was agreed that they should put up more sail and take a chance on getting into harbor before nightfall. Suddenly another towering wave smashed the shallop. The mast broke into three pieces and toppled overboard with the sail, in what was described as a "very grown sea." Working with great speed and diligence, the men cut away the fragments of mast and sail and thus avoided capsizing.

Then probably off the Gurnet, they realized their situation was not one to be envied. Relentlessly the wind, waves and incoming tide swept them along in the pitch blackness of the night. The roar of mighty breakers indicated land ahead. All aboard could see through the darkness the white surf rolling shoreward on a rocky beach. Mate Robert Coffin, who had been reassuring the others that he believed he knew where he was, now abandoned all hope.

Just as the shallop was about to be swamped by a giant comber, one of the sailors took momentary charge of the situation. Grasping his steering oar firmly, he shouted at his fellow seamen: "If you are men, about with the shallop, or we are all cast away!"

The others steadied their oars. Rowing with superhuman effort for about five minutes, they rounded a point of land I like to believe was Saquish, finally finding themselves in the lee of a large promontory. In the blackness of the night they decided to stay aboard the shallop rather than go ashore and face a possible attack by more Indians, which the Pilgrims called a "huggery."

Soon the wind shifted to northwest, and it became much colder. John Clarke, acting first officer, announced that he was going ashore anyway. He and several others soon landed from the rough surf. They lighted a fire, and one by one the others joined them and warmed themselves. When morning came they found that they were actually on an island (later named Clarke's Island for John Clarke) in Plymouth harbor. Exploring, the Pilgrims discovered a huge rock, which still stands on the island, and climbed to the top.

As it was then Saturday, they agreed to rest there, dry out their gear and conduct a service of thanksgiving on the rock, in which they would give the Lord "thanks for His mercies, in their manifould deliverances."

I like to think of this thanksgiving service at the giant rock as the first real Pilgrim Thanksgiving. I often visit the giant boulder, which still remains unchanged and unmoved, not like its sad companion, the famous Plymouth Rock, which has traveled many hundreds of feet and has lost many hundreds of pounds from its original weight.

Early on Monday morning, December 17, 1620, the Pilgrims sailed back to Provincetown in their repaired shallop and reported to the rest of the company that Plymouth harbor was their choice as the location for a settlement. And so it was that a party went ashore from the *Mayflower* on December 18, 1620, landing not very close to the large boulder on shore we have come to call Plymouth Rock.

CHAPTER 2

America's First Flyer

The name of John Childs should go down in history as the first successful American flyer or glider. There are two completely different accounts as to where John Childs was born: one indicates the North End of Boston in the vicinity of Unity Street, the other claims Europe as his place of birth but that he arrived in Boston early in life.

When Childs was quite young he became interested in the way birds fly. He would go down to the waterfront and observe in detail the flight of seagulls, ducks, sparrows and pigeons. He especially watched the actions of seagulls, studying them closely as they perched on the wharves, always facing the wind so that they would be able to fly successfully at almost any time.

As Childs grew into maturity, he developed many sound theories he was able to test later. He studied wind action and realized early that a good time to fly a kite was also a good opportunity to copy the birds and soar away into the sky, providing that his "wings" were of sufficient length and area.

In considering the possibility of a man flying compared to the ability of a bird, Childs decided greater areas of sail must be used for man to compensate for the difference in type of human weight to that of birds. Giovanni Borelli in 1680 proved that man's muscles were far too heavy and could not be compared to those of a bird. Childs offset this by making wings that were larger and longer in proportion to a human than the proportion of a bird's wings to its body. Probably Childs did not know that Leonardo da Vinci had drawn practical plans for flying. Otto Lilienthal used these plans successfully long after da Vinci and Childs were both dead.

It is possible that John Childs had heard of the tower jumping of the Marquis de Bacqueville. In 1742, just twelve years before Childs became active in the area around the Old North Church, the Marquis attached long wings to his body and leaped from his mansion near Paris to soar gracefully out over the Seine River. Unfortunately he landed ignominiously on a washerwoman's clothes barge anchored in the stream. Childs was an exception to most people attempting such a flight in that he never injured himself.

Gladstone Earl Millett of the Old North Church relates that Childs made his first descent without too much fanfare, landing successfully in a nearby field. On his second attempt he was greeted by scores of workmen and other Boston residents who had learned of his flight with admiration and wished to observe his next effort.

This time he took off from the Old North Church belfry, stretching wide his arms with their winged attachments to their fullest extent. A short time later Childs landed one hundred yards away in a field identified as in the vicinity of Henchman's Lane.

Finally the town fathers announced that since there was too much watching and not enough working because of the excitement of the flight, in the future no aviation of any sort would be allowed in Boston.

Hurrying to beat the date the edict would become law, Childs advertised that he would make the ultimate flight from the Old North Church. Not only would he fly, but he would be armed with two pistols which he planned to discharge on his way through the air from the belfry to the ground.

The appointed day, September 13, 1757, practically became a holiday, with hundreds of people from all walks of life assembled in the area where they believed Childs would make his descent. No one worked, it is said, within half a mile of the church.

Then came the moment when America's first flyer raised his wing-strapped arms, perched himself high on the edge of the belfry, watched his wings carefully as he unfolded them and leaped out into space. In the air on his way down he removed his two pistols from his clothing and fired first one, then the other, if we are to believe the records of the period.

Landing successfully once again, he accepted the applause of the thousands of onlookers in the North End. That was his last flight in Boston, for he vanished from the scene in similar fashion to the notorious Captain Gruchy, to whom a memorial still stands in the Old North Church auditorium.

The law against flying in Boston never has been repealed, and perhaps the residents of South Boston, East Boston and Winthrop may have some satisfaction in knowing that as far back as 1757 it became illegal to fly over Boston.

In 1923 the Colonial Dames erected a memorial to John Childs, and it stands today in the garden of the Old North Church. The Dames chose that year to erect the tablet because it was in May 1923 that the first nonstop cross-country airplane flight occurred, with John Macready and Oakley Kelly as the aviators.

The *Boston News-Letter* for September 8 to September 15, 1757, mentions John Childs and his daring feat. But did Childs really fire the pistols in midair as has been reported?

Here are the exact words of the *Boston News-Letter* article:

Tuefday in the Afternoon John Childs, who had given public Notice of his Intention to fly from the Steeple of Dr.

Cutler's Church, perform'd it to the Satisfaction of a great Number of Spectators; and Yefterday in the Afternoon he again performed it twice; the laft Time he fet off with two piftols loaded, one of which he difcharged in his defcent, the other miffing fire, he cock'd and fnap'd again before he reached the Place prepared to receive him. It is fuppos'd from the Steeple to the Place where the Rope was Fix'd was about 700 Feet upon a Slope, and that he was about 16 or 18 Seconds performing it each Time. As thefe Performances led many People from their Bufinefs, he is forbid flying any more in the Town.

CHAPTER 3

A Pig of Importance

Out of unimportant incidents come matters of great significance at times. Such was the case of the "sow business" in 1642, when controversy in the courts between the magistrates and the deputies cost a great deal in time, tempers and money. The dispute over the hog, trivial in itself, was responsible for the bicameral system of our government. After this court case was finally settled, the magistrates met by themselves as our senate does while the deputies constituted an independent house, thus establishing the two bodies in our legislature—the Senate and the House of Representatives. This system of government has lasted for more than three hundred years, and all because of a hog!

In 1636, when Sir Henry Vane* was governor of the Massachusetts Bay Colony, there came to Boston a traveling salesman, also called a drummer, who represented an English business house. His name was George Story, and he lodged at the home of a Mrs. Sherman. Story had samples from which to take orders. He hoped to get many orders in Boston, send them home to England and make a comfortable commission on his sales.

*Sir Henry Vane, whose statue is at the Boston Public Library, was later executed by having his head cut off in the Tower of London.

But Drummer Story was not welcomed in Boston. The Bostonians preferred to keep all business and all commissions among themselves instead of sending off to England. The merchants and magistrates of the area made it very unpleasant for George Story. They considered him most undesirable. There was a law against objectionable or obnoxious persons staying more than three weeks in town. When George Story overstayed this limit, he was brought before the governor upon the complaint of Captain Robert Keayne.

Captain Keayne was a prosperous merchant, a rich landowner and the first leader of the famous "Ancient and Honorable Artillery Company." He lived at what is now the corner of State and Washington streets. Like many highly connected men, he was often the object of ill will among the less wealthy, and at the time of this incident was under suspicion of extortion. In other words, he was also not universally popular.

George Story did not enjoy his encounter with the governor and determined to get even with Captain Keayne, the man who had caused his public discomfort. He decided he would wait until the perfect opportunity, which came in the form of a pig.

This pig belonged to Mrs. Sherman, at whose house Story boarded, and like most of its kind was of a roving disposition, very irresponsible, with the troublesome habit of running away whenever possible.

One day Captain Keayne saw this pig wandering along what is now State Street. He captured the pig and had it "cried"* through town. When no one claimed it, he put it into his own pigpen and gave notice that the owner could have the pig by proving its identity.

For some reason Mrs. Sherman never attempted to prove it

---

*The official town crier would make announcements through a small megaphone from various locations in Boston.

was her property or tried to identify it. When nearly a year had passed, Captain Keayne thought he had kept the pig long enough. As undisputed possession was ownership, he counted the pig as his and killed it for winter food.

That action was watchful George Story's opportunity for revenge. He knew of the whereabouts of Mrs. Sherman's pig even if she did not. As soon as the pig was killed, he induced Mrs. Sherman to believe that Captain Keayne had defrauded her of the pig by slaughtering it.

This was more than Captain Keayne, a magistrate of Boston, could stand. He objected to the accusations of Mrs. Sherman's friends that he was a pig murderer. He brought suit against both Mrs. Sherman and George Story for slander and defamation of character. The magistrates believed his story and fined Mrs. Sherman twenty pounds for damages.

George Story, realizing that events had not turned out exactly as he had planned but seeing an even greater opportunity for blackening Keayne's character, went about town telling Mrs. Sherman's sad tale, saying that it was outrageous that a poor woman be fined twenty pounds just because she had tried to obtain her just rights. Then he persuaded Mrs. Sherman to appeal to the General Court for justice and protection.

The General Court, the lawmaking and governing body of the Massachusetts Bay Colony, was the highest court of appeal, whose decisions were final. It was composed of nine magistrates, elected by the freemen, and thirty deputies, elected by the different towns. They all sat together—magistrates and deputies—in the General Court, and acted as a single voting and lawmaking body. The governor could not veto any decision.

Governor John Winthrop in his journal begins his account of the "sow business" with these words: "At the same general court there fell out a great business upon a very small occasion."

When Mrs. Sherman's appeal for justice because of the killing of her pig came to a vote, the Great and General Court was divided. Thanks to George Story's work among the people, the sympathies of the deputies were with Mrs. Sherman. But the magistrates were on the side of Captain Keayne. John Winthrop gives details of the voting:

> . . . the best part of seven days were spent in examining of witnesses and debating of the cause; and *yet it was not determined,* for their being nine magistrates and thirty deputies, no sentence could by law pass without the greater number of both, which neither plaintiff nor defendant had, for there were for the plaintiff two magistrates and fifteen deputies, and for the defendant seven magistrates and eight deputies, the other seven deputies stood doubtful.

Eventually it was decided by the court that the matter would be settled by Captain Keayne paying back the three pounds he had collected of the twenty-pound fine levied against Mrs. Sherman.

The actual importance of this dispute, which went on for years, is that it caused the wiser heads in the colony to see the impossibility of an elective assembly acting as a judicial tribunal. The deputies would most likely decide as the people who elected them desired, not necessarily as the real justice in the case demanded.

At last a compromise was arranged. The magistrates were to sit by themselves, the deputies by themselves. Each group would conduct its business separately, with new acts *approved by both* to become law.

This was the origin of the Massachusetts State Legislature.

The magistrates or assistants are the Senate, and the deputies are the House of Representatives, or the Assembly as it is sometimes called. And so the Great and General Court of Massachusetts was created in its present bicameral form because of a pig!

CHAPTER 4

America's First Aerial Photograph

An article in the August 1958 issue of *Flying,* entitled "Flashlight Lawrence," included a statement that Lawrence, "the first aerial photographer" of America, used balloons, kites and ingenuity when he took pictures from the air over the ruins of San Francisco after the earthquake of 1906.

The photographer may have operated as claimed, but one thing is certain: Flashlight Lawrence was *not* America's first aerial photographer. That honor rightfully belongs to James Wallace Black, a Bostonian. The article in *Flying* incorrectly asserts that the San Francisco pictures, made in April 1906, were the first air photos taken in this country. Actually, almost forty-six years before, on October 13, 1860, James Wallace Black took the first successful aerial picture in America from a captive balloon over Boston Common.

Black, whose earlier photographs of the construction of the present Minot's Light were masterpieces, had a studio in Boston at 173 Tremont Street, where he not only photographed the leading citizens of the day but also taught the science of photography to Oliver Wendell Holmes and many others.

Photography in the 1850s and 1860s was a very risky business, with perfect sunny weather necessary for outdoor pictures. Aerial photography was undreamed of until Black and a Providence friend, Samuel A. King, decided to attempt to make a picture of the Rhode Island capital from a tethered balloon high over the city.

The majestic *Queen of the Air* was the balloon they used. Although at first the day was bright and clear, wind clouds soon appeared in the distance. Black, working against time while high in the air, made a hasty attempt with the wet plates then in use, and a fair picture resulted. For a brief period of time the impression remained on the sensitized glass. But before permanence could be achieved, the storm clouds hit the balloon and the fixing material spilled and could not be applied. No more pictures could be attempted, for although the wind later diminished in strength, the clouds hid the sun for the remainder of the day. The first attempt at aerial photography had failed.

After careful organization of each minute detail of their plans, Black had the balloon brought to Boston, choosing Saturday, October 13, 1860, for the initial air photograph attempt over that city.

The project called for the balloon to take off from the usual location on Boston Common near the baseball diamond. The *Queen of the Air* soon soared aloft until it reached a position over what is now known as the Soldiers and Sailors Monument on the rise in ground then called Flagpole Hill.

When the balloon was tethered, it was arranged that a certain amount of its hydrogen gas would be released the instant a picture was made. Then, suspended about twelve hundred feet in the air, Photographer Black ordered the curtains lowered around the basket to simulate a dark room so that he could prepare his wet plates. Pictures had to be taken almost at once after the glass plates were treated with emulsion.

Immediately after the picture was exposed, he carefully treated the wet plate with the hydrogen, which blackened the picture to the degree desired. Then, when the sensitized glass was perfectly developed, he applied the fixing solution to make it permanent. His negative was completed as soon as it was dry.

During the next ninety minutes Black prepared, exposed, developed and fixed eight negatives in all. For many years it was believed that only one was a complete success. However, this was not so. Of the six that came out, some were blurred from the swaying of the balloon and two turned entirely black and were ruined because of an excess of hydrogen.

With eight negatives finished, James Black and his friend, Samuel King from Providence, untethered the balloon and for several hours enjoyed looking at the surrounding country as they drifted along. Riding the prevailing winds, they finally brought their trip to a close thirty miles away from the city, less than a mile from the sea and within a short distance of what is now Torrey Little's auction barn in Marshfield.

On his return to the city, Black made up prints from his favorite aerial negative of the Port of the Puritans. He found that the outer limits of the picture included the Old South Meeting House on the left, Boston harbor at the top, Summer Street at the right and Winter Street at the bottom of the photograph.

When I first saw this picture at the Old State House about half a century ago, I was intrigued. Several years later I was really fascinated when I located in a camera store* a sketch from the air on a glass slide of the area that apparently had been photographed by James Wallace Black that October day in 1860.

At first I thought that the original Black photograph had been copied by the artist who made the sketch or drawing.

---

*The store was Handy's on Bromfield Street, where they had hundreds of glass negatives and slides. Alton Hall Blackington had introduced me to the marvels of this institution.

However, a careful study of the artist's efforts revealed that there were areas in the sketch outside the known original limits of the Black photograph. It seemed to me that the artist could not have indicated the correct size and shape of the various buildings from the ground as they might have appeared from the sky, so the great question in my mind was how the artist could draw the sketch that had a larger area than Black's 1860 photograph.

I received a clue from Robert Taft's volume *Photography and the American Scene,* which eventually led to my discovery of another of Black's aerial photographs. I found that by putting the two pictures side by side, overlapping the new one slightly on the original, there is a much larger area and a better knowledge of the appearance of Boston at that time.

These two photographs are included in this book. They are oval in shape, as were many photos in those days.

The right-hand portion is the known photo; the left was taken almost immediately before or afterward, answering the question of how the artist sketched the area that was larger than the limits of the known picture.

In the foreground of the left photograph is the prominent Park Street Church, the Granary Burying Ground, a portion of the Boston Athenaeum where it joins the burying ground (in an arch, part of which is actually over the cemetery), the Tremont House, the Parker House, King's Chapel and cemetery, the Old City Hall and the Boston Museum.

Next is the Old State House, scene of the Boston Massacre. In the distance is the Custom House before the tower was added. To the left of the Old State House is Faneuil Hall and the Quincy Market. Following along Washington Street, the Old South Church can be seen.

Moving to the right of the double photo, Washington Street leads close to the Summer Street Church, which occupies a prominent position. This church was destroyed in the Great Fire of 1872.

Winthrop Square is easily discernible, with the scene of the Boston Tea Party at Griffin's Wharf outlined against several ships in the Rowe's Wharf area.

PART FIVE

Incredible Occurrences

CHAPTER 1

Latter-Day Jonahs

Many otherwise devoutly religious individuals have expressed doubt about the accuracy of the biblical account of Jonah and the whale. In similar vein, at least two 19th-century sailors are known to have survived after being swallowed by whales.

Peleg Nye, a Cape Cod whaler, used to recount his adventure to youngsters who visited his Hyannisport home during the 1860s. One of those children, Edward A. F. Gore, later of West Medford, told me the story in 1907 when I sat on his knee on our spacious piazza in Winthrop.

In March 1863 Nye fired his bomb lance into a sperm whale, and everyone aboard the longboat assumed that the whale had been killed. Nye prodded the huge mammal with a hand lance, and suddenly the whale slapped its tail and crashed its lower jaw into Nye's boat. Nye fell forward directly into the whale's mouth.

Scrambling to escape, Nye found himself trapped as the whale closed its great jaws. A sperm whale has teeth only in its lower jaw, teeth that fit into upper-jaw sockets. Nye was caught by the whale's jaws just below his knees, but the space between the whale's teeth and sockets was large enough to prevent his legs from being crushed.

The whale soon sounded. Nye believed the huge beast reached the bottom of the ocean with him before everything went black. Then Nye breathed in some seawater and lost consciousness.

Luckily, at approximately the same time, the whale gave up the struggle and floated to the surface, dead. Just before the mammal appeared, Nye's body came to the surface and was taken aboard the whaler. It was a long time before he could be revived, but he finally came to and recovered completely before reaching home. Living to the age of seventy-nine, Peleg Nye was known as the Jonah of Cape Cod.

An even more remarkable incident took place about twenty-eight years later—so remarkable, in fact, that the scientific editor of a Paris journal debated for 4 1/2 years whether to publish the facts in his possession.

Every facet was carefully checked and rechecked. Finally convinced of the truth of the story, editor Henri de Parville authorized its publication in the *Journal des Debats* on March 14, 1896.

On the afternoon of August 25, 1891, the whaling vessel *Star of the East* had come upon a great school of sperm whales. One of the whales, which had been wounded by a bomb lance thrown from a whaleboat, seized the boat in its jaws and crushed it in two.

The sailors leaped in all directions to escape. Steersman James Bartley jumped with the others, but just as he leaped the whale made a quick turn in the water, opened its mouth and caught the falling seaman. The other sailors saw the jaws close over Bartley. Giving him up for lost, they made their way back to the *Star of the East.*

Later in the day a dead whale came to the surface of the ocean. For two days the men worked at removing its blubber. When they finished, it occurred to one of the sailors that the whale they had been working on might possibly be the one that had swallowed Bartley.

After much discussion, the other whalers finally agreed to open the stomach and intestines of the immense animal. As they cut open the stomach, to their amazement and horror they saw the outline of a man through the membranes. Carefully slicing away the muscles, they uncovered the missing sailor, unconscious but still alive.

Moving Bartley with care, the sailors placed him on the deck, rubbed his limbs and forced brandy down his throat. His entire body had turned purple, and he was smeared with the whale's blood. Working on him in relays, the men soon had Bartley washed and his circulation restored. Then he regained partial consciousness. It was his hallucination that he was being consumed in a fiery furnace. Although the average temperature of a whale is 104°, this does not account for the terrible sensation the sailor experienced. Possibly it was caused by the constant pressure of the whale's body against his own.

The return voyage to England nearly restored his health. After he had a complete rest, he made this statement about his experience:

I remember very well from the moment that I jumped from the boat and felt my feet strike some soft substance. I looked up and saw a big-ribbed canopy of light pink and white descending over me, and the next moment I felt myself drawn downward, feet first, and I realized that I was being swallowed by a whale. I was drawn lower and lower; a wall of flesh surrounded me and hemmed me in on every side, yet the pressure was not painful, and the flesh easily gave way like soft india-rubber before my slightest movement.

Suddenly I found myself in a sack much larger than my body, but completely dark. I felt about me; and my hand came in contact with several fishes, some of which seemed to be still alive, for they squirmed in my fingers, and slipped back to my feet. Soon I felt a great pain in my head, and my breathing became more and more difficult. At the same time I felt a terrible heat; it seemed to consume me, growing hotter and hotter. My eyes became coals of fire in my head, and I believed every moment that I was condemned to perish in the belly of a whale. It tormented me beyond all endurance, while at the same time the awful silence of the terrible prison weighed me down. I tried to rise, to move my arms and legs, to cry out. All action was now impossible, but my brain seemed abnormally clear; and with a full comprehension of my awful fate, I finally lost all consciousness.

So improbable did the story seem that the captain and the entire crew of the *Star of the East* thought it necessary to give testimony of the incident under oath.

Bartley was about thirty-five years of age, strong in build and constitution. The only lasting effect of his terrible experience seems to have been a recurring nightmare in which he relived his sensations in the whale's stomach.

It might be well to review what the Bible says about Jonah. It is not claimed that Jonah was in full possession of his faculties for the three days he was in the whale. We know that he prayed, and then he probably lost consciousness, just as James Bartley did centuries later. To Jonah and his associates, a miracle had occurred:

And the Lord spake unto the fish, and it vomited out Jonah upon the dry land.

So we have the names of three men who have been in the jaws of a whale: Jonah, the son of Amittai; Peleg Nye of Cape Cod; and James Bartley of England.

CHAPTER 2

Rip van Winkle of the Blue Hills

From twenty miles out to sea, sailors in Boston Bay often sight the Blue Hills of Milton. For centuries the Indians of the area gathered in the hillside vicinity. Massachusetts Mount, as Captain John Smith called it, is said in folklore to have been one of the dead ice monsters that crawled down from the north with "stones on its back." Legend insists that all of these creatures were stopped when they reached the hollows dug by the sun god, the hollows that have become the beautiful New England lakes. There the gods pelted them with heated spears, melting the ice and leaving behind the glacial remains.

Big Blue, as it is called today, now boasts the Harvard Observatory at its peak. Three centuries ago it was relatively unpopulated, although at its base lived the Aberginians, a tribe said to be distantly related to the Indians on the Isle of Manhattan.

The chief of the Aberginians was Wabanowi, who "thought more of himself than all the rest of the people did." He doubled in brass as a medicine man, and he was a poor one. Before long, as his prophesies never came true, he was called "Headman Stick-in-the-Mud." The chief's daughter, Heart Stealer, was as beautiful as her father was stupid. The chief made it a point to nag her and to forbid her every wish, as he thought chieftains should do.

Then came the day when Fighting Bear, chief of the Narragansetts, visited Big Blue Hill and fell in love with the girl. He gave a long speech to Wabanowi, likening himself to the sun, the storm, the ocean and to all the strong animals he could recall. He compared Heart Stealer to a deer, a singing bird, a zephyr, the waves of the sea and flowers of the field.

Then, getting down to business, Fighting Bear asked for her hand in marriage. He went on with his speech, talking of the prophecy that a great race with "sick faces, hair on its teeth, thickly clad in summer and speaking with a harsh tongue" was soon going to drive the red man from the New England area. By this time, of course, the Indians knew that the whites had been living on the fringe of the great ocean not too far from Big Blue, but they had not caused trouble.

Stick-in-the-Mud, who considered himself the only prophet of the area, was outraged. Springing to his feet, he cried out: "Who has foretold this? I didn't. There is only one prophet in this district. I am the one. It isn't for green youngsters, Narragansetts at that, to meddle with this second-sight business. Understand? Moreover, my arm is so strong it needs no help to exterminate an enemy. I can beat him with my left hand tied behind me. Had Fighting Bear merely asked for my daughter, I would have given her up without a struggle. If somebody doesn't take her soon, I shall lose my reason. But Fighting Bear has added insult to oratory, and if he doesn't leave soon, he'll never get there at all."

Thus speaking, Stick-in-the-Mud wrapped his furs around himself so that only his nose showed.

Fighting Bear folded his arms, and with a scowl stated that his time would come. He then strode into the forest.

One evening not too long after this a heavy smoke developed over the Blue Hills, and shadowy forms were noticed flitting in and out of the smoke. All of the Indians now began to wonder what was going to happen.

Stick-in-the-Mud, who had been dozing as the smoke developed, awakened to find the spirit of a woman standing in the entrance to his wigwam. She beckoned for him to follow her. He did so at once, hoping to discover some secret that would be more useful to him than what he considered his fortune-telling matches, which usually ended in failure.

She quickly led him up a path of the Big Blue Hill. Finally they reached an outcropping of rock, and there was a cavern the Indian had never noticed before, although he had walked in the area on many occasions. The cavern glowed with a weird light, and Stick-in-the-Mud noticed that it was bedded with soft moss. Without knowing why, he sank on the bed of moss and watched, entranced, as the spirit began moving her arms in a slow, rotating motion. Soon he was sound asleep.

When on the next day his followers could not find him, they began searching the woods of the Blue Hill area but were unsuccessful. When the days turned into weeks and then months, his followers decided that he was not coming back, and elected another to take his place.

Down in Rhode Island, Fighting Bear heard that his tormentor had disappeared. He returned to the Blue Hills, where he again claimed Heart Stealer as his future bride. This time there was no one to object, and he took her back to the Providence area, where they were married.

As Charles M. Skinner tells us, now came the "men of sick and hairy faces, white men" who desired the earth and took it, making it no longer a place pleasant to live on. When war broke out, Fighting Bear and the other Indians fought valiantly but lost, and decided to keep the peace in the future.

Stick-in-the-Mud, back at the cave in the Blue Hills, awakened one day to find the cavern illuminated again, with the spirit that had taken him there standing over him. Noticing that he had awakened, she spoke: "Wabanowi, I caused you to sleep that you might be spared the pain of seeing your people forsake their home for other lands. The men with pale faces and black hearts are here. Had you been here you would have stirred them to break the peace and all would have perished. They have kept the truce. Now I set you free. Go into the Narragansett country and live with your daughter, who married Fighting Bear. Do not disturb their happiness."

The rock then swung open, and this Indian Rip van Winkle staggered out into the brilliant sunshine. His fourteen years of sleep had left him pained with rheumatism and covered with moth-eaten whiskers, which made the dogs in the area bark at him.

Stick-in-the-Mud looked down into the Neponset Valley, but all his followers had gone. Where his village had been were log houses and huts, and barnyard sounds could be heard. After gaining a little confidence, he descended from Big Blue and reached the Neponset River, where he shaved himself as best he could with a shell. An hour later he was on the road to Providence, arriving there the next morning.

He found the home of his daughter and Fighting Bear. Several of his grandchildren who were running around soon began playing games with him, in the most popular of which he served as a horse for the youngsters.

As the long Rip van Winkle-like slumber had rested him, Stick-in-the-Mud lived many years afterward. There are those who claim that he comes back once every summer to the Blue Hills area.

Every September, on the day nearest to a full moon, he appears at Big Blue and looks off at the sunset. You may see him then, or you may see him half an hour later skimming the surface of the Neponset River in his shadow canoe. Having thus visited the scenes of his youth, he retires for another year.

CHAPTER 3

Billy McLeod's Baby Seal

On Grape Island in Boston harbor lived Captain Billy McLeod and his wife as caretakers for thirty-four years. He had many, many stories to tell. One of the best concerns the tiny baby seal he found while he was strolling along the beach. Evidently the mother of the seal had been killed by one of the large boats in the area, leaving the seal to make its solitary way to Grape Island. Billy and his wife took care of the seal, feeding it carefully and nursing it along until it became quite frisky and was very attached to the couple.

In a short time the seal was performing feats of unusual agility. In the morning it would flip its way down to the shore, swim around for a time, then return to the house. When Captain Billy went out in his dory, the seal followed behind, always coming back with him.

Occasionally Captain Billy went to Boston, leaving his pet seal behind. When it was time for the captain to return, the seal swam out to meet him, was helped into the boat and rode back with him. Sometimes the seal reached the house before the captain, and there he knocked three times with his flipper as a signal that he wanted to enter. Once inside, he made a beeline for the stove, behind which a box had been installed. There he remained until suppertime. After supper Captain Billy put a little rug in the box, whereupon the little seal yawned in a knowing manner and curled up on the rug for the night.

The little seal finally died from eating green paint. Many children who had visited the pet mourned his death. Captain Billy said that although he had owned many pets since then, there never was an animal as affectionate as his little seal.

CHAPTER 4

Alice on the Bark *Russell*

One wintry night in 1907, when the snow was swirling around our Winthrop, Massachusetts, home and great icy flakes were beginning to bounce against the windowpanes, I watched and listened as Grandmother Caroline played the guitar to accompany Mother's zither.* As usual, I was fascinated at the speed with which Mother's hands flew over the zither strings.

As they often did during the long winter nights, Mother and Grandmother had promised to play some tunes after the dishes were done, for there was no television or radio in those days. Mother had interspersed the songs with stories of her unusual experiences on Robinson Crusoe's island and out on the high seas aboard the bark *Russell,* of which her father and my grandfather were captain.

For Mother, then Alice Rowe, her sea experiences began in 1869, at the age of eleven months, when she made her first trip on the *Village Belle,* captained by Grandfather Rowe. Eventually she learned to walk on that schooner. Later, when she went ashore, she found that she could not keep her balance because the land did not roll with the motion of a ship. Grandmother told me how she had to teach Alice to walk all over again.

*The zither was given to my mother in Chile, and she was taught to play it by a Dr. Harvey, an officer of a British frigate.

In the first five years of her life, Mother's parents were her only companions at sea, and they were her teachers as well. Grandmother Caroline instructed her in the usual school lessons and in guitar music and sewing. Grandfather Joshua Nickerson Rowe taught her how to box the compass, steer the ship and even "take the sun."*

When Mother and my grandfather would pace the deck every day for exercise, he told story after story of his career on the *Crystal Palace,* of unusual shipwrecks, pirate adventures and his Civil War service at sea. Often he would sketch pictures to illustrate his stories; thus Mother learned to make illustrations for the stories she wrote in letters to her cousins in Maine.

When Alice was fourteen she went on the English sailing bark *Russell* for 4 1/2 years, during which time she kept a diary or "log," as she called it. She told of the young stowaway Harry Kidd who became her companion as well as the cabin boy on the ship. She described the terrible feeling of watching in a wild storm as a vessel that had passed them was wrecked while the *Russell* was saved from striking the very same rocks only because the force of the wind brought the bark's fore lower topmast with its straining sail crashing to the deck, stopping their headway. One entry included her excitement when a whale came so close that when the ship rolled, she leaned over the rail and dropped a stick on the huge mammal's back.

Another entry told of the wonderful experience of passing through the Sargasso Sea. Her account of sailing around Cape Horn in a rough passage and finally seeing the Andes Mountains was most interesting.

While the bark *Russell* was in the harbor of Valparaiso, Chile, for repairs, her father called Alice and her mother into

---

*Using the quadrant to assist in finding the position of the ship.

the chart room and asked, "Where do you think we are going, young lady?"

She guessed wrong several times and finally gave up. Grandfather Rowe smiled and pointed to the chart of the South Pacific Ocean. "We are going," he said, "to Robinson Crusoe's island."

His statement astounded everyone.

Alice asked, "Father, did Robinson Crusoe really live near here, and isn't it a made-up yarn anyway, like *Little Red Riding Hood*?"

"No, it is not," replied Captain Rowe. "His real name was Alexander Selkirk, and he lived on the island of Juan Fernández, 360 or more miles west of this city. I have promised to take a freight of two masts to the island for a small ship they are building there."

After a three-day sail with a fair wind all the way, those aboard the bark *Russell* saw a great purple cloud on the horizon, which gradually changed to what appeared to be a huge pile of rocks. As they sailed nearer it proved to be a towering mountain peak called the Anvil,* 3,040 feet high. The island spread along the horizon for about fifteen miles.

When the ship reached the anchorage, a boat came out to the *Russell* carrying Count de Rodt, governor of the island, who brought fresh vegetables and goat's meat as a gift. Captain Rowe showed him around the ship, after which Alice and her father and mother were invited to go ashore with the governor and explore the island.

On one of their trips around the island they went to see the cave that Alexander Selkirk had lived in for the four years he was alone on the island. In a small boat they skirted the foot of the tall cliffs, sheer rock walls towering over 1000 feet. Sud-

*The Spanish name is El Yunque. Convicts were given their freedom if they climbed it. Few succeeded, most falling to their death.

denly they sighted a tiny beach. Captain Rowe guided the craft in on a big rolling wave, the boat rushing up on the beach at a dizzying rate. After climbing out of the boat they walked along the shore and up a path that led through a natural tunnel in the cliff until they reached the famous cave of Alexander Selkirk.

The room inside had been dug from solid earth. Shelves scooped around the sides held dishes and other household articles, while a hammock slung from side to side made the cave look homelike.

Several days later they made a trip to the great lookout where a tablet had been erected to Selkirk's memory. It was truly a perilous journey. After making their way through a wooded area with many burrs that stuck to them, climbing over huge rocks, inching over a narrow ridge with yawning gorges on each side, they finally reached the top. Alice lay down to rest. Suddenly she heard her father's voice: "I am monarch of all I survey! My right there is none to dispute; from the center all around to the sea, I'm lord of the fowl and the brute!" From the topmost point he recited William Cowper's poem, "Alexander Selkirk's Soliloquy." Then Captain Rowe read aloud the tablet, which stated that Selkirk was landed at Juan Fernández from the *Cinque Ports Galley* in 1704, and after four years and four months of solitude he was taken off by sailors of the privateer *Duke* on February 12, 1708.

Captain Rowe decided to try to find a shorter path to return to the governor's home. Plunging into a forest with beautiful ferns and moss clinging to the trees and rocks, they eventually found a brook running toward the sea and followed it for a time, until it plunged over a fifty-foot precipice. After scouting around they located a tree they thought might bend, as it was fairly slender and yet strong. Pushing, shoving, rocking it back and forth, they managed to bend it down until two of the

younger and more adventurous members of the party scrambled over and forced the top of the tree to the bottom of the cliff,
where they held it. Everyone crawled down the trunk except the
dog Jess. It seemed she would stand there barking and wagging
her tail forever, but Jess suddenly decided to take a chance and
started coming down the bare, steep cliff. When she reached the
bottom her paws were torn and bleeding. Meanwhile the governor had sent a rescue party for them. My mother always told
this story very dramatically and closed it with the question,
"Did we climb up that tree or down it?"

Another adventure began when the party from the *Russell*
were rowing along at low tide near the foot of the cliff and saw
a black space with a deep opening. Alice wrote of her experiences that day:

> "Now," Father ordered, "do just as I say. Pull hard at
> the oars and duck down your heads. I'll steer."
>
> We did as he commanded, and in we shot, finding our-
> selves in a beautiful cavern! The flickering light was danc-
> ing over the interior with a blue tint, caused from the
> sunlight striking down through the azure depths of the
> water and reflecting up into the cave. It seemed like fairy-
> land.
>
> The roof was high inside, like a church, and hung down
> in pinnacles of rock. It extended in about a ship's length,
> and we could hear the waves breaking on a little beach.
> The water was the most brilliant blue I ever saw, and was
> filled with bright yellow fish. . . .
>
> Our boat was soon made fast, bow and stern, to some
> jagged rocks, then out with our lines, and what sport we
> had. The fish were not a bit afraid of us or our lines.
>
> I became so excited catching them so rapidly that I
> made my line shorter and shorter, and still on they came,

until finally I was just holding the baited hook in the water, and they bit as fast as they could!

Then I proudly said: "Watch me! I am catching fish by just holding the hook in the water, without any line!"

I had hardly finished saying this when the boatman shouted in a voice of terror: "Look out, Miss Alice!"

I jumped and snatched my hand out of the water, and as I did so a pair of jaws came together with a snap!

"Well, young lady," said Father, "you just escaped having your hand bitten off. In the future never fish without a fishline! That was a water snake or a young sea serpent about five feet long. I guess we had better get out of here as fast as we can if we have stirred up a nest of those creatures."

We cast off our mooring lines and started for the mouth of the cave. There we found we were in a trap, as the tide had come in while we were fishing and the entrance was too small for the boat to go through.

But we had Father who always found a way to do what seemed impossible. . . . As the boat was higher than the overhanging rock, one side had to be tipped under the edge and pushed along while we all lay flat on the slimy fish. First one side of the boat, then the other, was tipped, and while we were tipping it we kept thinking, or I did, that if we upset we would be thrown in among all those water snakes with jaws full of big sharp teeth like a wolf's! . . . It was luck that we tried to get out of the cave before the tide was any higher, for we just managed it and that was all . . . What a supper the cook gave us that evening! Those yellow-tailed fish were delicious fried in salt pork and eaten with island vegetables. I was pretty glad to be eating cave fish instead of cave fish eating me!

*   *   *

Another exciting incident aboard the *Russell* was the shooting of a sea lion, which was brought aboard when it was supposedly dead. As it lay on the deck with everyone gazing in wonder at the huge creature, it rose up on its tail and roared, chasing first one person and then another. Finally Harry, the cabin boy, grabbed a sledgehammer and took it up into the rigging. After tempting the beast to come toward him, Harry waited until the animal was directly below and then, with a mighty blow, struck the sea lion on the head. This time the creature was really dead, to the relief of the captain and crew. If you know how an inchworm moves, you can imagine the sea lion walking, only instead of taking an inch at a time he took eight feet.

On the final trip of the *Russell* with Captain Rowe in charge, the bark was to sail for England with a load of manganese ore. They stopped in Chile on their way and had another adventure in which the dog Jess was the hero. Alice and her mother were wandering along a brook some distance from the rest of the party when Jess began to whimper and whine. She crouched down near Mrs. Rowe while looking intently at a large bush farther up the stream. When the bush started to move and Jess trembled even more, Alice's mother said she believed that the dog could smell some wild beast. Having heard that when in such a predicament one should never turn his back and run, she and Alice walked backward with one of them always staring at the bush until there was a turn in the brook and the bush was out of sight. Then, dropping the flowers and ferns they had been collecting, they raced to the shore, where they found the captain talking to a native fisherman. They blurted out their story and were told that the dog had saved their lives, as there were lions in the vicinity. Later, after two children had been carried off by lions, a big hunt was organized to make it safe for the people. Alice vowed never to wander in the woods again.

CHAPTER 5

Treacherous Harbor Ice

I was born in Winthrop, Massachusetts, which is almost entirely surrounded by water. On two occasions I nearly lost my life when the harbor froze over and then started to melt.

The first experience occurred when I was about ten years old. Winthrop had run out of coal, and the emergency supplies that had been trucked in were being sold to those who could transport the 100-pound bags from the Town Hall to their homes. It was my job to fetch the heavy coal bags the 2 1/2 miles to our residence high on Cottage Hill. Weary after walking all the way over to the center, I decided to take a shortcut across the ice of the inner harbor on my way home.

I thoroughly enjoyed this part of the trip until I reached some rubbery ice and fell through with my sled and the coal. With great effort I managed to climb out, and even salvaged my sled with the coal just as I was about to give up. I trudged over the ice more warily the rest of the way and then, after climbing the hill to our house, told my adventure to my family. I have always wondered whether the joy expressed upon my safe return was over the saving of the boy or the coal.

On January 2, 1918, I spent the morning hiking around on the ice of Boston harbor. Toward afternoon, because of the rising temperature, I came to some rubber ice and suddenly found myself up to my armpits in the frigid water, which was far over my head in depth. There was no one around for miles. It was then about three o'clock in the afternoon and the temperature was below zero. I could feel my rubber boots rapidly filling with water.

The rubber ice kept breaking as I fought to crawl up on it. After resting a moment by hanging onto the edge, I began a furious battle to escape. Kicking my water-filled boots in the best trudgen stroke I could muster, I clutched at the edge, gaining ever so little at times and then falling back as the ice gave way under my weight.

Again and again I fought for freedom, but each time my efforts seemed to be successful the ice would break and I would find myself back in the water up to my armpits. The air trapped in my pea jacket somehow prevented me from sinking below my shoulders.

With my sixth try came the realization that I was making some progress. Although the lower part of my body still broke through the ice, I was able to work my shoulders farther out of the water. Gradually I was able to raise my body until my waist reached the edge of the broken surface. Anxious not to lose this hard-won advantage, I continued kicking frantically, at the same time taking care not to batter the ice with my legs. Meanwhile my fingers clawed deeper into the frozen surface and I achieved another slight gain.

A moment later I worked myself out on the ice as far as my waist, and then did a quick turn of the body, rolling the remainder of my torso free of the hole. In order to keep my weight distributed as much as possible, I made three more rolls away from the spot that had trapped me. Then I stopped. I lay there breathless, just a few feet away from the narrow thirty-foot-long stretch of water I had opened, hoping I had won the fight.

I began the long, tedious trip to the safety of Apple Island. Not daring to stand erect, I rolled over and over, making probably seventy-five revolutions in all. In this awkward fashion I reached Apple Island, only to realize that trouble still lay ahead. I had half a quart or so of water in each rubber boot and knew that even if I could pull the boots off I could not get them back on again without help. I was about two miles from home and the icy weather, still far below zero, was getting colder. This was the time to prove how good a runner I was. Racing down the hill on the Cottage Park side of Apple Island, I started with great lumbering strides to cover the distance to my home.

The ice was good and solid the whole distance to the area near the Winthrop Yacht Club where I had scrambled down on the frozen harbor hours before. When I reached the mainland the sun was setting. Four minutes later I was safe at home.

I learned two things from these experiences: how treacherous harbor ice can be, and never to travel across its surface without taking special precautions. In 1936 seven boys acquired the same knowledge in an even more frightening and dangerous way.

On the afternoon of Sunday, February 9, 1936, seven boys, all from Rhode Island, on leave from their Civilian Conservation Corps camp at East Brewster on Cape Cod, started out to walk across the ice to Wellfleet, despite the warnings of their friends that the warming trend would break up the ice field.

They were later sighted three miles out by Hudson Ellis, who watched them through a telescope from his Cape Cod home. To his horror, he saw the ice on which they were walking break away from the main field. The boys continued to walk, however, unaware that they were marooned. In fact, as the youths later explained, darkness was falling before they discovered their plight.

Ellis immediately notified Lieutenant Julian Kavier, in charge of the CCC camp, who in turn summoned the Coast Guard.

A Coast Guard plane from Salem, piloted by Lieutenant True G. Miller, was sent out at once. Also dispatched were three Army bombers from winter maneuver base at Concord, New Hampshire. They were joined by a private plane from Boston, piloted by Captain William Wincapaw, for whom I took over as the Flying Santa at Christmas that same year.

Major Giles, pilot of one of the Army bombers, spotted the seven lads on two drifting ice cakes seven miles out in Cape Cod Bay. Notified of their location, the other planes dropped food and blankets to the marooned group.

Finally, after having been adrift for twenty-two hours, the boys were brought aboard the cutter *Harriet Lane* through the heroic efforts of Coast Guardsmen who braved death by pushing and rowing lifeboats through the ice field.

Two youths were rescued from a small ice cake, the other five from the main cake. All suffered from exposure, having been tossed about all night at the mercy of ice, sea and wind. One, John E. Fitzsimmons, Jr., nineteen, of Portsmouth, had both his feet frozen and needed medical treatment. The others rescued were Manuel J. Botello, nineteen, Albert M. V. Papa, eighteen, and Tony Ray, eighteen, all of West Warwick; Nicholas S. Scungio, eighteen, and Norman R. Beaulier, eighteen, both of Pawtucket; and Thomas G. Malone, nineteen, of Portsmouth.

Unable to make the East Brewster shore because of a solid blockade of ice, seven feet thick in places, the *Harriet Lane,* accompanied by the faster Coast Guard patrol boat *Argo*, ready to take off any of the young men if a medical crisis arose, headed for Provincetown on a three-hour run. Aboard were seven boys who, like myself, had learned the hard way the treacherous nature of a walk on the ice.

The *Britannia* Sails on Time

New England is known for its variable weather and cold winters. In the old days the harbor froze over more often and more solidly than it does now. Whatever the reason—propeller-driven motors, pollution, more marine traffic or warmer weather in recent years—the water of the inner harbor does not freeze solidly as far as the docks at the present time.

Perhaps the most interesting ice episode in the entire history of Boston Bay concerns the Cunard liner *Britannia*. One day late in January 1844 the liner arrived safely at her pier in East Boston, and that very night the harbor began to freeze. With the steamer scheduled to leave soon after February 1, it became embarrassing to the merchants and residents of the city when the ice grew thicker and thicker. Because of maritime rivalry, the people of New York would never let the Bostonians live it down should the *Britannia* be prevented from sailing because of the ice.

On January 30 Mayor Brimmer presided at a meeting to decide what could be done. Matthew Hunt was appointed to cut a channel to liberate the *Britannia*. After working all through the bitterness of a blustery winter's day, Hunt found that the ice was freezing faster than he could cut it. He notified the committee that he could not fulfill the contract.

John Hill and Gage, Hittinger & Company then agreed to cut

the channel. Professional icemen with much experience on the ponds and lakes of Massachusetts, they recruited a large force of expert ice cutters, who soon assembled to begin the work.

Thousands of eager citizens in holiday mood went out to watch the ice cutting on February 1 and to visit the tents and booths set up by enterprising individuals. Boat Keeper Berry, one of the Boston harbor pilots, walked up to the town from Gallop's Island. Men with ladders charged a cent each for eager harbor explorers to reach the ice from the sidewalk level of the city. The men had cut holes around the public landing stairs to prevent citizens from getting on the ice in their own way without paying for the privilege.

The *Boston Journal* of February 1, 1844, reported the method of cutting the ice:

> A channel of about sixty feet in width is first marked out, which is then divided into blocks of about thirty feet square. The sections marked are then *ploughed,* by which the ice is nearly cut down to the water. The plough used for this purpose is formed of seven different ploughshares, perfectly flat, and very sharp, which are arranged in a row, nearly similar to what is called a cultivator. After ploughing, the ice is sawed, so as to detach the cakes entirely from each other, after which two grapnels are attached to the cakes and they are hauled under the stationary ice by a gang of about one hundred and fifty men, some fifteen or twenty men standing on the cake in order to sink it sufficiently to make it pass under.
>
> The blocks of ice on one side only are thus disposed of, thus forming a channel of thirty feet in width. The blocks on the other side are to be detached after this channel has been finished, and will float out to sea with the ebb tide.

The work was kept up hour after hour, and even an injury to contractor John Hill, hurt jumping from a cake of ice, did not delay proceedings. By late the next afternoon the work was completed, and the *Britannia* was assured of being able to sail the following day.

On the morning of February 3 the adventuresome inhabitants of Boston made their way to the waterfront, where they went down on the harbor ice to watch a spectacular event: the sailing of the Cunarder *Britannia*. Several hundred people viewed her moving away from the pier. Backing into the slot in the ice cut for the purpose, the *Britannia* turned her paddle wheels until the prow faced the open channel. Slowly moving her engines, the beautiful vessel sailed out through the artificial channel while at least two hundred cheering enthusiasts walked alongside all the way to Castle Island, where they gave the *Britannia* a noisy and colorful farewell.

PART SIX

Shipwrecks

CHAPTER 1

The *Home,*
Lost Off Ocracoke

The story of the *Home* is the type of steamer disaster that holds public attention for many years. When a ship goes down with her crew, it is surely considered an unfortunate event. But when a passenger craft goes down carrying great numbers of men, women and children from all walks of life, the awesome dangers of the sea are brought home to everyone who learns of the catastrophe.

The paddle-wheeler *Home* was launched in April 1836 from Brown and Bell's yard in New York. Her owner, James B. Allaire of New York, was proud of the fact that the *Home* was among the fastest craft of her day. Unfortunately her 22-foot beam proved wholly inadequate for her 220-foot length.

All went well on the *Home*'s maiden voyage from New York to Charleston, South Carolina. On her second trip the *Home* broke the speed record between the two ports, negotiating those stormy coastal waters in an amazing sixty-four hours.

Following this swift journey there was talk that after a few more trips the *Home* would be groomed for a spectacular ocean crossing. The merits of the vessel were so widely discussed that whispers of doubt as to her safety were dismissed with a tolerant but contemptuous smile by her owner, Mr. Allaire.

On the afternoon of Saturday, October 7, 1837, the *Home* was scheduled to sail from New York to Charleston. Excitement over the voyage reached a feverish pitch. Many who had not planned to make the trip were carried away by the enthusiasm of the crowd and boarded the vessel in New York. Possibly fifteen persons sailed on the *Home* who failed to give their names to anyone ashore. Because of this, the total number of persons on board the *Home* was never definitely known. It is certain, however, that there were forty-five in the crew and ninety identified passengers, of whom about forty were women and children. James B. Allaire, the owner's nephew, was among the passengers, for his uncle had certain theories about the performance of his vessel that he wished to have tested on the high seas.

At exactly five o'clock the crew removed the gangway. Farewells rang through the air as the paddle wheels began pushing the *Home* seaward. Passing through the Narrows, the steamer was proceeding at better than twelve knots. When she reached the new Captain Gedney Channel, the pilot was confused by what was then known as the Romer Buoy, and the steamer grounded heavily on a shoal. She hung there for more than three hours until the incoming tide freed her. Then, after a private conference between Mr. Allaire and Captain Carleton White, the steamer proceeded down the bay.

Drawing abeam of Sandy Hook Light, the *Home* veered to starboard and began her long trip toward distant Charleston. On and on the paddle wheels carried her, until by Sunday morning there was much talk among the passengers and crew of a record passage between Sandy Hook and Charleston.

That evening the wind changed and came strong from the northeast. The waves built up to ten feet in height. After a few violent wrenchings, the steamer began to take in water. The storm grew in force and intensity. By midnight the *Home* was wallowing in the dangerous seas of a mighty gale, a predicament for which she had never been built.

The rolling, pitching and straining of the ship soon weakened the engine bed, slowing down the paddle wheels. Whenever a wave caught the *Home* under her port guardrails, the ship listed sharply to starboard. This threw the port paddles out of water, where they vibrated alarmingly as they turned uselessly in the air. Sometimes it was ten or twelve minutes before the captain could bring the *Home* around and get the ship back on an even keel.

James B. Allaire was much embarrassed by this turn of events. He had made the journey to satisfy his uncle that the *Home* could reach England, and here she was in difficulty on a trip from New York to Charleston. He retired to his stateroom and did not appear for hours.

The crew set emergency sails on the masts, which steadied the ship for several hours. But after sunset Sunday the storm grew more intense. The seams in the hull widened and the water streamed in. It required the entire crew to keep the pumps from losing their battle with the sea. Despite their frantic efforts, around midnight the water in the hold began to climb, slowly but inexorably. Inch by inch it rose, until Captain White was so frightened that he sent out an appeal for help to all ablebodied men. Hand basins, buckets, pails, chamber pots and pans were called into service as bailers. Many of the panic-stricken women volunteered for duty. In spite of everything, the water rose higher and higher.

With the coming of dawn, the bleak, forbidding shores of Cape Hatteras were seen ahead. Soon Cape Hatteras Light was visible twenty-three miles away. Captain White ordered the course changed so that the *Home* would clear the terrible reefs surrounding Hatteras Island, and before long the lighthouse faded from view. By two o'clock in the afternoon it was agreed that the danger of hitting the shoals was over. A new course was chosen to bring the *Home* nearer to land. Captain White decided he would beach her on the nearest shore if there was no other safe alternative.

Hour after hour the *Home* had been weakening and working loose. By this time every successive wave was actually tossing the bow three or four feet from the rest of the vessel's framework! Soon the entire hull began to work up and down, bending and twisting as though it were a deckload of laths that had been swept overboard.

This sickening motion roused terror among the passengers. Many gave up all hope of survival and consigned themselves to their Maker. Others made desperate preparations to save themselves, cutting blankets into long, thin strips with which to secure themselves to spars or timbers when the ship went to pieces. The two life preservers on the boat had been appropriated by two men, and the *Home* carried just three lifeboats —sufficient for only half the number of passengers.

At six o'clock Monday night water reached the engines; they gave a final vibrating quiver and died. In the strangeness of that unexpected silence, every passenger felt that the end could not be far away. Beyond sight of land, the ship was running before the wind with her emergency sails. Without the engines, her speed was more than halved.

Shortly before nine o'clock that night the storm clouds broke, revealing the moon shining eerily. By its pale light the distant shores of Ocracoke Island were visible, and soon afterward it became clear enough to see the welcome flashes of the island's lighthouse.

Captain White decided to beach the *Home* at Ocracoke and gave orders to the helmsman to that effect. Nearer and nearer the straining side-wheeler came toward the beach. Soon the moonlight revealed close at hand the glistening backs of the great waves as they hurled themselves up on the shore. Captain White ordered all hands to prepare for a violent shock when the 220-foot vessel hit the sand. By ten o'clock the *Home* was in the outer breakers. Soon a mighty wave worked itself under the stern, lifted the *Home* high amidships and sent her forefoot crunching to pieces as she struck bottom more than four hundred feet from the island.

There was instant chaos and confusion. Above the noise of the breaking timbers could be heard the desperate shouts of men, the high shrieks of women and the children's piteous cries of terror. The *Home* settled into the sand and began to break up. Mr. Allaire had come out on deck some time before to talk with Captain White. After a hasty conference, they ordered the women and children forward so that they would be nearest the shore. The screaming and wailing continued, with husbands and wives clinging together and children clutching their mothers. The gale-force wind pushed the giant billows through the weakening structure of the *Home* and on toward the shore, where they broke with a thunderous crash.

By now most of the women and children had reached the forecastle. Several waves swung the *Home* around until her bow was at an angle toward the beach. Then a tremendous comber began to rush toward the doomed ship. Catching the women and children on the forecastle, the wave pulled them all into the ocean together. All but two of the women drowned almost at once. Only one of the children, a boy of twelve, was thrown up on the beach alive.

The two women who survived could be seen clinging desperately to fragments of wreckage as they floated toward the island. Mrs. LaCoste of Charleston, an elderly woman who was so heavy she had trouble walking, had lashed herself to a deck settee before the wave washed her off the forecastle with the others.

Shipwreck news always travels rapidly, and as Mrs. LaCoste struggled feebly toward land, the islanders were there waiting for her. Each wave pushed her closer to them, until finally a giant wave caught the frightened woman and carried her along at an alarming speed. As it broke against the sand, it swept Mrs. LaCoste high on the shore. When it started to recede, the undertow began to pull her out to sea again. At that terrifying moment the islanders rushed into the surf and rescued her.

Out on the wreck of the *Home* plans were made to launch a craft into the sea. The jolly boat was put over and three men jumped aboard. Before they could push off, a wave caught the boat and capsized it, drowning all the men. Another wave then snapped the lines and sent the empty jolly boat to crash on shore. The longboat was dropped into the sea and twenty-five passengers scrambled aboard. Another great wave caught and capsized the longboat; every one of the twenty-five persons perished.

A short time later large fragments of the paddle-wheeler began to break away from the hull of the vessel. Many of the braver men attached themselves to the floating timbers; a few reached shore safely. The *Home*'s smokestacks began to totter shortly afterward. The port stack fell just as a woman passed beneath, carrying her baby toward the upper deck. Both mother and child were killed instantly.

A Mrs. Schroeder of Charleston had lashed herself to a deck-rail brace. When a wave swept her overboard, she dangled there, submerged with each passing wave. Mr. Vanderzee of New York noticed her helpless position. Reaching down over the side, he seized her by the clothes and held her up for some time, but was unable to pull her over the rail. Finally the strain proved more than he could stand, and he was forced to release her. As she dropped into the water again, the brace gave way. When a wave caught her and threw her up on the shore, she frantically dug her feet into the sand and clung to the brace. Despite her efforts, the undertow pulled her halfway down the beach. Still tied to the brace, she rolled up again before the next great billow thundered on shore and engulfed her. Time after time she was swept almost above the high-tide mark, only to be dragged out by the next sea. Her strength was rapidly ebbing. Just as Mrs. Schroeder lost consciousness, a summer visitor at Ocracoke, a man named Littlejohn, rushed into the water and saved her.

By this time Mrs. LaCoste and Mrs. Schroeder were practically naked. Gently the islanders carried them up the beach and covered them with sand as protection against the cold. They were later taken to the home of William Howard on the island.

Out on the *Home,* the Reverend Mr. George Cowles of Danvers, Massachusetts, was struggling to help his wife to safety. The well-known minister always had experienced a "strong and invincible dread of the sea" but was persuaded to take the voyage because of the fast passage of the *Home.* While helping his wife reach the ruins of the quarterdeck, he met Steward David Milne, son of a minister. Placing his hand on Milne's shoulder, he comforted him with a verse from the Bible: "He that trusts in Jesus is safe, even amid the perils of the sea." As he finished speaking another great wave swept across the forecastle, and when it was gone both the Reverend Mr. Cowles and his wife had vanished.

The *Home*'s forecastle snapped off a short time later. On it were Captain White and seven men. They floated ashore safely. Of the estimated 150 persons who went aboard the *Home* in New York, twenty passengers and twenty of the crew survived.

By noon they found themselves "among a set of savages" from Ocracoke Village. Several families did everything in their power to help the survivors. These benefactors included the Howards and the Wahabs, leading families on the island. Before the end of the week, the forty survivors had been taken by inland water craft toward their respective destinations.

In all, twenty bodies from the *Home,* including that of Mrs. Cowles, washed ashore and were buried by William Howard in his cemetery.

It is easy to criticize a sea captain after a disaster. Several passengers from the *Home,* led by a Mr. C. C. Cady, claimed that Captain White was intoxicated most of the journey. However, Steward Milne quickly came to the captain's defense and praised him warmly.

"Captain White drank only two glasses of absinth cordial all the time during the trip," said Milne. "It was a passenger, Captain Alfred Hill, who was drunk, and others confused the two. Captain White didn't eat, sleep or lie down in his office until he was entirely worn out by fatigue and watching day and night at the wheel."

At the time of the disaster India rubber life preservers were just coming into use. There were only two aboard the *Home*; both carried a passenger ashore. One of these survivors remarked that had the side-wheeler been supplied with 150 life belts instead of two, there would have been fewer deaths that October day in the violent surf off Ocracoke Island.

CHAPTER 2

~~~~~~~~

In Memory of the *Pamir*

The German sailing ship *Pamir,* which was closely associated with the great commercial house established by Ferdinand Laeisz, has now been at the bottom of the sea for some time. In the last few years of her existence, this steel four-masted bark made headlines whenever she arrived in port or sailed away. She was a commercial, deep-water, wind-propelled vessel, one of the few survivors of her rig afloat.

To many who followed the sea either as a profession or as a hobby, a mention of the *Pamir* would reawaken memories of the days of old, bringing back names such as shipping experts Robert Hilgendorf and Reederei F. Laeisz. The long, glorious history of the Laeisz sailing ships of Hamburg, Germany, is not as well known as it should be. These great German sailing vessels, many of them using the initial letter *P* in their name, set many important records.

It was a dramatic sight when a Laeisz ship sailed into a crowded anchorage. The motto of the "Flying P" was, as Laeisz stated, "My ships can and will make rapid voyages." And indeed they did. Shortening sail as they neared port, seamen would also be rigging cargo gear and opening hatches to get ready for quick handling of the cargo even before the anchor rattled down. The departure of a Laeisz ship also was accomplished with similar speed and economy of motion.

Along with such craft as the *Preussen, Potosi, Padua* and *Passat,* the *Pamir* was beloved by millions. The 3150-ton four-master was a solid craft. Built in 1905 at the Bloehm and Voss yards in Hamburg, she seemed destined to live forever. During her half century on the high seas, she had survived World War I without trouble and had weathered many gales.

Obtained by the Italian Government in 1924, the *Pamir* later was sold to Gustav Erickson of Finland, owner of a large fleet of sailing ships. He would not have bought her, together with her sister ship the *Passat,* unless he considered her outstandingly seaworthy. Both these reliable sailing ships plied the Australian run. They brought wheat and other goods to Europe, earning substantial funds during an eight-year period.

When World War II began, the *Pamir* fell into British hands. Impounded and registered in the New Zealand navy, she served for a time as a school ship. During the war the bark made six journeys to the west coast of America. Next, a British grain importer chartered her for four years, putting her in the Australian corn cargo business. Then, although there was an acute shortage of merchant shipping at the time, the British company gave the *Pamir* back to Erickson.

A Belgian salvage company bought the *Pamir* and the *Passat,* outbidding the shipbreakers. Meanwhile, West German groups insisted that the two ships should be acquired for training German marine officers. Their reason was that a first-class German marine officer, in order to qualify for a position, had to have sailed as a boy in one of the big windjammers. People began to ask about a new German mercantile marine, wondering where the future captains and officers would come from if there were no more sailing ships in which they could learn the ropes and get their training.

Shipping regulations in Germany still required that a candidate for a helmsman's papers and even a master's certificate must have done a certain amount of training in sailing ships whose total area of canvas was at least twice the ship's length, considering the beam. The *Pamir* and the *Passat,* each with a minimum area of canvas of about 2800 square meters, met these requirements—and there were no other qualified German craft.

Finally a Hamburg shipowner named Schlieven bought both craft. After having them modernized, he engaged them as cargo sailing ships to train future officers of the merchant navy. Thus the *Pamir* and the *Passat* were brought back to Germany, were refitted and were soon equipped with all the latest devices.

And so it was that the *Pamir,* carrying a 900-horsepower Krupp-Diesel engine as auxiliary, sailed under the German flag again after thirty-eight years. On January 10, 1952, she left Hamburg on her first voyage, bound for Rio de Janeiro.

Almost before she was out to sea she encountered trouble. At the eastern entrance to the English Channel during a storm, the screw of her auxiliary engine fell off and an anchor was lost overboard. The storm developed rapidly, turning into a gale that gave the forty-nine cadets aboard a real taste of excitement and danger. They watched as two British ships came to the *Pamir*'s aid. When she put over her remaining anchor and the flukes caught, the immediate danger was averted.

Better weather soon followed. Nevertheless, the incident reminded the older officers of an earlier disaster that ended in death at sea for many German sailing cadets. On February 8, 1938, the Hapag training ship *Admiral Karpfanger,* a 2853-ton four-masted steel bark of Hamburg, had sailed from Port Germein, South Australia, for Falmouth, England, with forty German sailing cadets aboard. She was never heard from again.

In 1952 the *Pamir* experienced no further incidents of danger en route to South America. After thirty-four days on the ocean she sailed into Rio. Necessary repairs had been made at sea, and as she came up the bay the beautiful German training ship with her smart young cadets received a tumultuous welcome.

When the *Pamir* reached Rotterdam at the end of her second

South American voyage—October 30, 1952—she was impounded by a Dutch ship's chandler, for Schlieven was in financial trouble. Not only had he sunk all his capital into purchasing and refitting the two sailing ships, he had also amassed a considerable number of other debts. Since his vessels were not earning the amount of money he had expected, the inevitable happened: a bank foreclosed. For two years the *Pamir* and *Passat* remained at their moorings.

A *Pamir* and *Passat* fund was set up in 1955 to enable the two craft to sail the high seas again. Sufficient money was raised to buy them, and both were put into service in 1956 as training ships.

On June 1, 1957, the *Pamir* sailed from Hamburg on her sixteenth round trip to the Argentine. At this time she was one of the most stable sailing ships that ever put to sea, with six watertight compartments, new steel masts and sixteen-millimeter iron plates.

Captain Hermann Eggers, who had already made seven trips in the *Pamir,* had planned to command the voyage, but a sudden family crisis made him go on leave. In his place sailed Captain Johannes Diebitsch, a mariner with extensive knowledge and experience. When the *Pamir* started back to Europe from Buenos Aires in September 1957, the ship was supposedly in perfect shape and there was no apparent cause for anxiety.

The good summer sailing weather came to an end abruptly. On September 20 Captain Diebitsch received warning of a hurricane, which the United States Weather Bureau had christened Carrie. It is believed that Diebitsch then attempted to sail around the storm.

Contrary to all expectations, Carrie did not veer to port as normal hurricanes do. Instead, the mighty gale headed for the central Atlantic and caught the *Pamir.* The tall-masted ship, under full press of sail and on a northerly course homeward at the time, was battered to such an extent that she was unable to ride out the blow.

What will always be an unsolved mystery is how Captain Diebitsch and Chief Mate Rolf Dieter Kohler planned to meet the situation when they realized Hurricane Carrie was going to catch them. We shall never know; neither officer survived, and the logbooks went to the bottom with the *Pamir.*

On board the sailing craft was Captain Fred Schmidt, a writer of sea stories. For years he had taught in the navigation school at Lübeck. Schmidt signed on for this particular voyage to take pictures for an illustrated work he was writing about life in oceangoing sailing ships. His last letter, written an hour before leaving Buenos Aires, is full of enthusiasm for the vessel and her crew. He was already looking forward to publishing the photographs and articles at the end of the voyage. The hurricane caught the *Pamir* that Sunday evening, and all Schmidt's plans for the future ended abruptly.

The first the world knew of the trouble was on Sunday, September 21, 1957, at 1500 hours Greenwich time. The *Pamir* sent out an SOS that she was struggling desperately in a heavy gale. Her position was given as 30° 57′ North, 40° 20′ West. She stated that she had a 45° list, was in danger of sinking and had lost all her sails. The British coast radio station at Portishead rebroadcast the message at once so that all available craft could reach the scene.

Ships within a near radius hurried to the general location after receiving the SOS. The closest of all was the American freighter *President Taylor.* Her radio operator announced to the world that she was making full speed for the *Pamir* and hoped to arrive at the scene at 2300 hours that night.

The Canadian destroyer *Crusader* then radioed that she would arrive at the same general location within twelve hours. The *Manchester Trader,* a British steamer, picked up an SOS and immediately relayed it to all other stations. Shortly after this the *Trader* received a broken message stating in part that the *Pamir* had met trouble and had her ". . . foremast smashed by the heavy sea."

Nothing further was ever heard from the *Pamir*'s radio.

Other craft announced their plans and positions. The British tanker *San Silvester* signaled that the *President Taylor* was due at the scene at 2300; the *Penn Trader* was expected to arrive at the same time. The Norwegian motor tanker *Jaguar* was 160 miles north-northwest, making eight knots. The German motor ship *Nordsee* was making ten knots and the British motor ship *Hauraki* was proceeding at fifteen knots. The *Tacoma Star* and the Dutch oceangoing tug *Swarte Zee* also started for the sinking *Pamir*.

At eight o'clock that Sunday evening the *Pamir*'s captain had received final warning that a hurricane could be expected within two hours. A survivor explained what occurred when the hurricane warning was announced:

> We were given orders to secure all rigging. All hands were sent aloft, but before we could start taking in sail, the hurricane overwhelmed us.
>
> Captain Diebitsch's order to trim sails came too late. A mighty squall tore the foresails away, and the mast snapped. From that moment disaster followed disaster. Things went so quickly that no one could say exactly what happened. The power of the storm forced the ship over on her side. We took on a 30° list, which increased to 35° and finally to 40°, the limit of the instrument's recording device. Of course, by this time the decks and holds were awash. The order "All hands on deck" was given. We all put on our lifesaving jackets; the ship heeled over more and more, shivering beneath the weight of mountainous seas. No longer could we get a foothold on the almost vertical

deck, and it was impossible to lower a lifeboat with this heavy list. We held on fast to the rail on the starboard, for the port side was already underwater.

When our ship suddenly capsized, we plunged down into the water, one after the other. Many of the boys must have been drowned at this moment. Those with any strength left attempted to swim away, but the suction of the ship drew us after her. Our only thought was to get away from her.

Now it was every man for himself. Small groups reached pieces of wreckage, to which they clung. There were fifteen men in my group. At last we sighted an empty boat drifting ahead of us. It took me an hour to swim to it, and only nine others reached it. We clung fast to the boat while the heavy seas broke over us. After long weary efforts, we managed to climb into the lifeboat, which was full of water, kept floating by its ballast tanks.

Meanwhile, shortly after eleven that evening, the *President Taylor* and the *Penn Trader* arrived at the position the *Pamir* had given. Of course they did not know if it was correct. In the dark, stormy night it was extremely difficult for the two cargo boats to find the damaged vessel. They cruised about the area looking for the sailing craft or survivors of the shipwrecked crew.

The *Tacoma Star,* a Blue Star Liner, now arrived on the scene. A few minutes before midnight, lights were sighted in the distance by the *Penn Trader,* but she was unable to find the *Pamir.* Soon after this lights appeared at another location, then disappeared also. The report of sighting flashing lights traveled around the world, arousing new hopes. Since the *Pamir*'s radio had become silent, it was feared she had gone down with all hands. Throughout the night searchlights from four ships shone constantly, shifting back and forth across the water but revealing nothing of the cadet ship. Hours went by. Shortly before dawn the Canadian destroyer *Crusader* arrived to help in the search.

The world hoped that the *Pamir* might have been driven before the storm with her radio out of action. A broken foremast, which the *Pamir* had announced, was no reason to fear the worst. But the *Pamir* had reported a 45° list as well, the real cause for alarm.

When daylight came, the air-sea rescue squadron on the Azores and the Coast Guard cutter *Astacan* began a systematic search of the sea west and northwest of the Azores. Bad weather and poor visibility finally forced them to abandon their efforts. It appeared that the *Pamir* had disappeared with all hands, leaving not the slightest trace to tell of her fate.

At noon the next day the British Coast Guard station at Portishead in Somerset, England, relayed a message from the tanker *San Silvester* that she had sighted an empty lifeboat and taken it aboard. Badly damaged, it bore the name Lübeck, the *Pamir*'s home port. The rudder of the lifeboat was still lashed inside, and it was apparent that it had been washed overboard. Two more lifeboats were sighted that afternoon, but the stormy Sunday came to an end without a single member of the crew having been found.

Then came good news. Late that night the American freighter *Saxon* sighted a lifeboat. As they drew closer, the watchers counted five sailors aboard, actually the surviving members of the ten who had clambered into the craft some hours earlier. The boat was full of water; it could not be bailed out because of the overwhelmingly rough seas and stormy weather. Details of the rescue of these five fortunate survivors were relayed all over the world. It was now definite from what the cadets told their rescuers that the *Pamir* had foundered in Hurricane Carrie.

The survivors said that only a small number of the crew had been able to take to the boats. Just two lifeboats were available because of the terrible list on the *Pamir.* They explained how their five companions had washed overboard, one by one, unable to retain their hold. The survivors estimated that there had been twenty-five men in the second lifeboat. Her lights had been sighted briefly just before the five men had been rescued, and they guessed the second boat could not be far away.

Strangely enough, twenty-four hours went by without a single report concerning the other craft. Meanwhile, it was erroneously announced by a careless radio operator that forty survivors had been rescued.

The ships kept up their hunt for the remaining sailors and cadets. Finally the United States Coast Guard cutter *Absecon* sighted the missing lifeboat. Sadly, only one man was in her. He was quickly rescued.

The sole survivor told a dramatic story of how the others had panicked into swimming to a waiting vessel whose men did not see the lifeboat. The ship seemed just a short distance away, but when they leaped into the water and started to swim, she steamed off, slowly at first. With all twenty-four men in the sea swimming desperately, the vessel gathered speed and disappeared into the gathering darkness. All twenty-four drowned as the remaining occupant of the lifeboat watched helplessly. He was the last survivor to be saved. Eighty-one men lost their lives.

What was the reason for the disaster? According to Quincy historian John R. Herbert, one theory is that the captain was too slow in shortening the canvas, and the ship went over. Another thought is that the *Pamir* was a very sensitive ship, and although she "could go like the dickens," she did not have a deep keel and could easily tip over.

In his scholarly book *The Set of the Sails,* Alan Villiers

mentions both the *Preussen* and the *Potosi,* stating that they were "magnificent spectacles and great pieces of sailing ship engineering," but "were probably poor things aerodynamically." When Villiers speaks of aerodynamic problems, he is probably referring to the difficulties of shortening sail quickly when a sudden storm comes, as well as the problem of wind pressure on the rigging, masts and spars of a square-rigger even with her sails furled. "Going under bare poles" is a term often used when a ship hits a storm and has her sails secured.

The usual square-rigged hull was not a deep-keel ship resembling a Gloucester fisherman. The square-riggers usually had hulls more like steamships. The problem of wind ships in storms often came when skippers, in an attempt to prove their craft could make fast runs, waited too long to shorten sail and thus suffered disaster.

The tragedy of the *Pamir* shows the problem of handling sail in a storm. The testimony of the few survivors indicates they did not have sufficient time to shorten canvas. Thus the ship rolled over and sank.

The people of Lübeck have preserved the lifeboat of the *Pamir* at St. Jakub's Kirche as a memorial to the lost cadets. The battered sides of the lifeboat, which carried many of the cadets after the *Pamir* sank, still show the jagged and splintered timbers that speak of the violence of the cruel sea. The lifeboat has become a shrine of remembrance, erected by the parents and relatives of the lost crew. Over the sides of the craft are draped scores of triangular black pennants, each bearing the name of a lost cadet. Covering the walls of the alcove are wreaths from many maritime nations offering messages of condolence, together with inscriptions from parents and relatives of those lost, commending their sons to the mercy of God.

CHAPTER 3

Plundering the *Howard* and the *Persia*

The wreck of the *Howard* in 1807 and of the *Persia* in 1829 have at least two common bonds: both were plundered, and neither received the historical notice they deserve. Sidney Perley of Salem, whose volume *Historic Storms* is everywhere cited for its detailed analysis of shipwrecks in general, missed the two vessels completely. Years later Bruce D. Berman ignored both wrecks entirely in his *American Shipwrecks*. Joseph E. Garland in his 1971 book *Eastern Point* was the first author to make an adequate report of the two Cape Ann wrecks, although I had mentioned the *Howard* and briefly recounted the story of the *Persia* in my 1943 volume, *Storms and Shipwrecks of New England.*

A much earlier writer, the Reverend Dr. William Bentley, kept a stupendously effective diary from 1784 until his death in 1819, in many instances far surpassing Samuel Sewall in the fullness of his entries on marine subjects. His first mention to any extent of storms at sea was made in 1786:

22 . . . Capt. Jona. Mason junr being obliged on account of the Ice to anchor in Nantasket Road, was carried upon Point Allerton by the breaking up of the Ice, & in securing the Vessel, the Mate (37) lost both legs & this week died.

Although there were countless shipwrecks and other disasters before the turn of the 19th century, the first marine calamity on Eastern Point of which any real details have come down through the years was the loss of the ship *Howard,* at a point less than two hours away from her Salem home.

The storm was mentioned by Bentley as the "loss of an India ship belonging to Mr. W. Gray of this port in sight of our lights & off Cape Ann, worth 100 th. D." The details were included in several newspapers, and the residents of the North Shore soon learned of the tragedy.

A strong northeast storm was sweeping across Cape Ann's rocks and beaches, buffeting the *Howard* as she neared the end of her lengthy voyage from Calcutta. Suddenly the lookout high in the rigging spied breakers ahead, indicating that the *Howard* was in dire trouble. But he had no chance to alert the crew. A moment later, as Grape Vine Cove came into view, the three-masted vessel broke her back almost at once and began to smash to pieces on the rocks of Cape Ann.

No identifying light had warned those aboard the *Howard.* A great wave hurled Marblehead Captain Bray, his mate and two sailors over into the terrifying combers then hitting the rocks. Those still aboard the broken ship tied themselves on the quarterdeck, but they soon yielded to the elements and were pulled off the ship and into the stones and rocks of Grape Vine Cove.

At first no one on shore knew of the wreck of the *Howard,* but soon endless material was belching forth from the sea, piling up on the beach in such confusion as only a terrible shipwreck can produce. Crowds soon lined the shore to salvage what the sea had provided for them.

As great bales from the cargo washed open, the folk along the rocky beach fought for the valuable goods and cloth, often using knives to detach pieces of material from the main bale, with cuts and bruises to show for their efforts. It is easy to criticize poor people for taking goods from a disaster along the coast, but there was little else in the wintertime to produce any sort of revenue. The Reverend Dr. Bentley gives a succinct review of the situation in his diary entry for March 4, 1807:

4. The shipwreck at Cape Ann has not given a higher opinion of Cape Ann than we have been taught to hold of Cape Cod. The disposition to pilfer was not easily restrained even by guards, and if we cannot prevent thefts at fires in our best towns, we cannot preserve our goods scattered on the shore when the storm is over. Much must be allowed for description, but after many deductions, pilfering is a sad vice when it has any excuse for it or any temptation to it. The Law must have a lash to it & the soldier can only execute it. It is said an offer of 5th D. was made for the savings & if they exceeded 7th D. all above that sum was to be returned to the Owner.

It was not too easy for even the minister to be definitely sure that taking goods from a wreck was wrong in all cases. He writes again in his diary on March 17, 1807:

17. Dr. Phelps of Cape Ann Harbour, assures that sufficient evidence had been obtained that the charges respecting the pilfering of the Shipwreck cargo belonging to the Ship Howard were false. That the principal articles of value missing instead of being plundered were concealed in the piles on the shore by the persons employed to collect the remains in hopes that being sold on the spot they might profit from the concealed articles, & that the truckmen had been discovered as privy to such secret villainy. . . . The

most aggravated charges were at first brought against the inhabitants.

Several of the tricks resorted to by the thieves are worthy of mention. One thief filled a bag with loose hay and then was chased over several acres of land by a sentry, who caught the thief, a local rogue named Jack Low. As the guard was emptying the bag, containing merely hay, Jack Low vanished. How much important material Low obtained by running back to the wreck we shall never know, but it probably was substantial.

The remaining wreckage was loaded on carts to be brought from Gloucester back to Salem. The caravan of wagons was stopped by a tree that lay across the road, the drivers getting down to lift the tree out of the way. When the task was completed, the driver of the last team returned to his wagon to find that every parcel of goods had been stolen. The rogues of the area, indeed fast workers, may have felled the tree as part of their scheme.

We do not have the sagacious Dr. William Bentley to record the loss of the brig *Persia* in his diary, for he died in 1819. But the newspapers were reporting in much more detail in 1829, when the *Persia* was lost with all hands on the night of March 5.

Captain Thissell of the *Persia* and his mate Nathaniel B. Seward were both from Beverly. The brig had been loaded with rags at Trieste for Salem. A violent easterly storm caught them in the darkness off Cape Ann, a very short distance from Cape Ann Light.

Although the wreck of the *Howard* had indicated the need for a spindle or lighthouse at Cape Ann, nothing was done until 1828, when the government took action to erect a daytime marker to replace the venerable oaks that had been markers for centuries. No man could touch these natural markers by order of the government, but the trees died one by one, and efforts at replacing them failed. A daytime marker was agreed upon, but before it was constructed the *Persia* was lost with all hands. Five months later the beacon was erected.

It was snowing thickly that night of March 5. The *Gloucester Telegraph* tells us that a watch in the pocket of the steward stopped at about eleven-thirty, indicating that the brig went down about eleven. The *Persia* had cut in too close to the Point in the heavy snow. Whether or not the daytime beacon was in place would not have made the slightest difference. There was actually no visibility, making it impossible to help those aboard. As far as is known, they perished almost at once in the breakers.

Nine bodies were eventually found, including the captain, mate, cook and steward. All were easily recognized. The longboat came ashore untouched, causing many of the people of Gloucester to believe that the crew had tried to get ashore in the boat, a belief fortified when one smart sailor found that there were marks where the gripes had been cut. The five unidentified bodies were buried from the Reverend Mr. Jones's Meeting House, and a goodly representation of sailors marched with the dead crewmen to the cemetery.

Certain marks on the unknown bodies were recorded, including the letter "I" inside the left arm of one victim. Another had an "L" on his stockings. A third, who was about five feet four, had a large scar on his right cheek and four doubloons in his pockets. Two more of the crew were later discovered firmly wedged in the rocks, requiring the efforts of no less than six men to extricate them. There were probably thirteen aboard.

The *Salem Courier* reported that the rags from the *Persia* were sold at auction, adding that if they were left at Western Point they would be "certainly stolen." The *Gloucester Telegraph* did not let the remarks of the Salem paper pass unchallenged, stating that if "our inhabitants are more dishonest than our neighbors in cases similar to the above, we doubt."

CHAPTER 4

A Brave Dog to the Rescue

Artist Winslow Homer made a tremendous impression when he presented his first exhibition. To a generation of art lovers and critics who were familiar with importations from the Continent, his efforts must have appeared gross, stark, imposing, even austere. His picture entitled "Saved" depicts the rescue from the *Harpooner,* with the breeches-buoy, the sailor and the pregnant mother.

Prominent in the disasters along the Newfoundland coast is the tragedy of the British transport *Harpooner,* hurled to her doom in 1816. Aboard were 385 men, women and children returning from Quebec to London after the War of 1812. Most of the passengers were attached to the Fourth Veteran Battalion of the British Army, and there was also a canine passenger on board. Before leaving Quebec the *Harpooner*'s master, Captain Joseph Bryant, had purchased a fine Newfoundland dog he named King. By the time they were a week at sea the captain and the dog were close friends.

On Saturday morning, November 9, 1816, the *Harpooner* was proceeding on her course past Newfoundland when a violent gale of snow and rain hit the area. Soon the mighty seas were pushing the transport off her route toward the great cliffs of Saint Shotts. At eight o'clock that night the second mate's watch was called, and an hour later came the cry dreaded by all sailors: "Breakers ahead! Breakers ahead!"

A moment later the *Harpooner* hit heavily and then slid off that reef, only to crash against another. The vessel began to fill and settled over on her larboard beam, half submerged but supported by the rocky ledges surrounding her.

In the midst of these disastrous events the dog King rushed up to his master and seized his coat sleeve, pulling him in the direction of the cabin. The dog was just in time, for the cabin was ablaze from several lighted candles that had overturned on impact. Captain Bryant, with the help of a dozen sailors, soon put out the flames.

A short time later a mighty wave picked up the *Harpooner,* lifted her completely off the ledges and sent her wallowing in the heavy seas closer to shore. All was now hopeless confusion. Many men, women and children rushed up on deck; scores of others drowned in their cabins.

Again the ship hit on a gigantic undersea ledge and lodged there fast on the rocks. This time the masts were toppled by the force of the blow. Several passengers tried to float ashore on them, only to be dashed to death at the foot of the cliffs.

By four o'clock the next morning, when the storm seemed to let up, Captain Bryant had to devise some way of getting his passengers ashore. He knew that the *Harpooner* could not stay afloat much longer. As the first step in his plan he asked his mate, Mr. Hadley, to take four men in the jolly boat and try to reach a rock on shore.

Ten minutes later the men pushed off in the jolly boat. Several giant waves swept in and nearly capsized them, but finally they managed to reach the shelter of a huge rock one hundred yards away from the *Harpooner.* Just as they were about to land, the jolly boat was smashed to pieces under them. The five men scrambled to safety and soon climbed onto the highest point of the rock. There they discovered that the rock was still a good distance from the shore. Nevertheless, it was so high that they would be safe indefinitely.

Mr. Hadley now shouted across to Captain Bryant, "Let your log line float in so we can secure it." The captain signaled to show that he understood. Soon the log line began to drift in toward the rock. It came closer and closer. Then suddenly the current swept it away from the rock. Time and again the log line was rereeled and let over, but always the current proved too strong.

Parts of the ship were now breaking off and drifting toward the rocky shores. Captain Bryant realized that at any moment the *Harpooner* might break up altogether and that all on board would be lost. Then he had an idea born of desperation.

Calling his dog King, he tied the log line to the animal's collar. Then he pointed to Mr. Hadley on the rock. "Go get him!" shouted the captain.

A moment later King sprang from the rail into the sea.

From his perch on the rock, the first mate began whistling and shouting to the dog. Fifty yards from the ship, King encountered a heaving mass of wreckage that swept him under the surface of the sea. When he emerged, he had a small timber caught in the log line. King seemed to be having difficulty breathing, and Captain Bryant ordered the dog pulled back to the ship. The order came just in time, for King was choking because of another fragment of wood twisted between the line and his collar.

"I'll know better now," said the captain. Removing King's collar, he looped the log line around King's shoulders and secured it with a bowline. On the signal to jump, King sprang into the swirling seas again and made for the rock where the mate was waiting with his men. This time King swam much more easily, and the men played out the line rapidly as he neared the rock. Soon he was caught in a giant swell. With a mighty crash he was pushed high up on the rock within a few feet of the waiting men. But before they could reach him, the undertow snatched the dog back into the raging ocean at the foot of the cliffs.

When the next wave broke the men were ready. The mate had locked arms with the others, forming a human chain. As King was again lifted high on the rock, he swept in past Mr. Hadley, who made a frantic try for him and missed. As the undertow began to pull the dog out again, the log line came in near enough for the mate to grasp it. "Hold on," he shouted. The men fought with all their might to prevent the deadly undertow from carrying King back into the ocean.

For a split second it seemed that both men and dog would be dragged out into the boiling sea, but the sailors clung desperately to the rocky crevices on the ledge. A moment later the men were able to pull King to safety.

The mate shouted to the captain that King had made it to the rock with the log line. The captain now tied a heavier line to the end of the log line and signaled ashore for the sailors to pull away. Finally the heavy line reached the rock. The sailors then retrieved from the sea enough timbers to build a makeshift tripod. When the tripod was secured to the rock, several of the *Harpooner*'s crew decided to attempt swinging hand over hand along the hundred yards of line between the ship and the rock.

The *Harpooner* had struck at nine o'clock Saturday night, November 9. It was almost Sunday noon when the first sailor swung out and started for shore. He landed on the rock amid cheers from the other survivors. A short time later a block was rove on and a sling arranged. One by one the survivors were hauled up onto the huge boulder. Only one passenger who attempted the trip failed to gain the rock. This unfortunate man was struck by a gigantic wave as he swung out onto the line, lost his hold and fell to his death in the ocean.

Each trip in the sling took ten minutes. Late Sunday afternoon there were still over 140 people left on the ship. Since the storm seemed to be dying down, several of the men decided to risk throwing themselves into the sea and swimming for shore. Most perished immediately.

Around four o'clock Sunday afternoon it was decided that the women should try to ride the sling. The first woman to make the attempt was a soldier's wife who was expecting a child at any moment. Her husband was placed in the sling first in order to hold her in his arms, and then the trip shoreward began.

All eyes were upon the couple as they moved slowly toward the rock. The survivors watched tensely as a wave swept over the pair. When it had passed, they could see that wreckage had caught in the block. The next wave freed the line, however, and the soldier and his wife neared the great rock where the men waited to help them. Now the most difficult part of the task was at hand: hauling the double load up the face of the boulder.

The men on the rock went down the line hand over hand to reach the couple, now almost submerged by the surf. Finally they succeeded in pulling the husband and wife to safety. Less than two hours later, sheltered from the wind and spray by the other survivors, the soldier's wife gave birth to a baby boy.

By now the situation on the *Harpooner* was desperate. The vessel could not last much longer. The sun had set and there were still more than one hundred survivors waiting to be taken ashore. At seven o'clock Sunday night the heavy rope, frayed by constant working and swinging across the sharp rocks, snapped in two. There was no way of replacing the line, and many gave themselves up to despair. The tide slowly rose again, great waves sweeping over the wreck. The *Harpooner* was going to pieces.

The first break came around midnight at the stern. Then, at four o'clock Monday morning, the *Harpooner* split in two up to the forecastle. In the mad scramble for safety, dozens were swept overboard to their death. Captain Bryant stayed aboard his ship until almost the last, when a gigantic wave caught him and pulled him under. He was never seen again.

The very last person to leave the broken vessel was an old subaltern, Lieutenant Mylrea of the Fourth Veteran Battalion. Over seventy years of age, he remained on the vessel until everyone else had either been rescued or lost. Then he thought of his own life and leaped into the sea. Miraculously, he floated to the rock and was pulled to safety. Of the last one hundred aboard the *Harpooner,* over fifty drowned.

The 177 survivors remained on the rock until dawn. The men were able to start a fire, and they carried the soldier's wife and baby near its warmth.

Low tide at daybreak, November 11, 1816, allowed five men to wade ashore. A mile away they found the home of a fisherman. They were taken to Trepassey, and by Wednesday evening, November 13, all but five of the survivors had reached that town to be billeted in the homes of the good people there. Near the wreck at Saint Shotts, in the fisherman's house, the soldier, his wife and the newborn baby were recovering from their terrible experience. All survivors reached Quebec the following spring.

In the tragedy of the *Harpooner* 208 persons lost their lives. King, the dog, was responsible for saving more than 155 of the 177 survivors.

CHAPTER 5

A Whale Sinks the *Essex*

Several years ago I made a pilgrimage to Pittsfield, Massachusetts, and the surrounding area where Herman Melville lived. His *Moby Dick* is, of course, one of the great literary classics in the English language, and the passing years have enhanced his reputation as a master of literature.

Melville's own career was exciting. Born in New York in 1819, he later sailed aboard a whaler to the Marquesas, where he deserted and was captured by cannibals. An Australian ship rescued him. After returning to America he wrote several books built around his experiences among the man-eating natives. In 1851 he finished writing *Moby Dick*.

At first the book failed to receive acclaim. But literary experts gradually came to appreciate the novel's merits, and when the author died in 1891 it had been accepted as a great work. In the years since his death, *Moby Dick* has established a permanent place in the world's great literature. There are several interesting and little-known facts in the background of events that led Melville to write *Moby Dick*.

In May 1839 Jeremiah N. Reynolds, an author whose name time has obscured, published in *Knickerbocker* magazine a story entitled "White Whale of the Pacific," about a whale named Mocha Dick. A summary of this tale, and excerpts from it, appear in this chapter.

Reynolds's words concerning the American whaler show his deep interest in the profession:

Yet vast as the field is, occupied by this class of resolute seamen, how little can we claim to know of the particulars of a whaleman's existence!

That our whale ships leave port, and usually return, in the course of three years, with full cargoes, to swell the fund of national wealth, is nearly the sum of our knowledge concerning them.

Could we comprehend, at a glance, the mighty surface of the Indian or Pacific Seas, what a picture would open upon us of the unparalleled industry and daring enterprise. . . . You are ever upon the whaling ground of the American seaman.

A group of those same American seamen mentioned by Reynolds met on the island of Nantucket one day early in August 1819, the year Melville was born. They were good neighbors and were planning a whaling voyage to the South Pacific. The meeting was called to sign the papers that would launch their journey. Each person who contemplated joining the long expedition of about three years duration put his name to the document.

SHIPPING PAPER

It is agreed between the Owners, Master, Seamen, and Mariners of the Ship *Essex* of Nantucket, George Pollard, Jnr. Master, now bound on a whaling voyage in the Pacific Ocean and elsewhere

That in consideration of the shares affixed to our Names, we the said Seamen and Mariners will perform a Whaling Voyage, from Nantucket, and return to the said port of

Nantucket. Promising hereby to obey the lawful commands of the said Master, or the other Officers of the said Ship *Essex;* and faithfully to do and perform the Duty of Seamen, as required by said Master, by night or by day, on board the said Ship *Essex,* or in her Boats; and on no account or pretence whatever, to go on Shore, without leave first obtained from the Master or Commanding Officer of said Ship *Essex:* Hereby engaging, that forty-eight hours absence, without such leave, shall be deemed a total desertion.

And in case of disobedience, neglect, pillage, embezzlement, or desertion, the said Mariners do forfeit their Shares, together with all their Goods, Chattels, &c, on board the said Ship *Essex:* Hereby for themselves, heirs, executors, and administrators, renouncing all right and title to the same. And the Owners of said Ship *Essex* hereby promiseth, upon the above conditions, to pay the Shares of neat proceeds of all that shall be obtained during said Voyage, agreeable to the Shares set against the names of Seamen and Mariners of the Ship *Essex* as soon after the return of said Ship to Nantucket as the Oil, or whatever else may be obtained, can be sold, and the Voyage made up by the owners of said Ship *Essex* or by their agent.—

In Testimony of Our Free Assent, Consent, and Agreement to the Premises We have hereunto set our Hands, the Day and Date affixed to our Names.

The master of the vessel was the first to affix his signature. His first mate, whose pen was later to give the world a classic account of the dangers of whaling at sea, was the next to sign. Then, one by one, the others planning to make the voyage affixed their signatures.

It was the twelfth of August that year when the *Essex* sailed

from Nantucket Island. Known as a three-boater, she was registered at 238 tons and had a relatively small crew. The size of
the crew was not important, however, as almost every man
aboard was a specialist in his field. Captain Pollard planned to
lower his own starboard boat; Owen Chase, mate, would lower
the larboard or port boat, while Second Mate Matthew Joy was
in charge of the waist boat. It was the men who were thoroughly
versed in their occupation who made the great hauls. The crew
aboard the *Essex* had carefully studied the habits of whales and
discovered their many feeding grounds.

The course of the ship was charted accordingly. She sailed
for the Western Island Grounds, after which she cruised for a
time in the Saint Helena and Tristan da Cunha areas. She
rounded Cape Horn and arrived at Santa Maria Island in Chile
the following January.

Santa Maria, mentioned by Reynolds in his tale of Mocha
Dick, had been used for many years as a post office for whaling
vessels. The *Essex* planned to drop outgoing mail and pick up
news from other Nantucket whaling vessels.

Whaling that year was good along the Chilean coast, and by
the time the season ended the *Essex* had the equivalent of 1000
barrels of oil. Thus in one-third of her time out, she was half
filled. The men were jubilant, expecting a quick trip home with
relatively high profits.

After stopping at the port of Tumbes on the South American
coast, Captain Pollard aimed his vessel for the Galápagos Islands to pick up turtles for food. Down through the centuries
pirates, buccaneers and whalers all had gone ashore here to take
aboard large numbers of these edible creatures. After about 300
turtles of varying weights had been brought out to the *Essex,*
the ship sailed to Charles Island, where another sixty turtles
were caught.

Neither at Galápagos nor Charles had whales been sighted.

Captain Pollard surmised they had not yet reached that point in their annual migration. Arriving at the equatorial grounds, the *Essex* soon began to sight spouts. She reached longitude 119° West, just below the equator and about halfway between the Galápagos and the Marquesas.

A day long to be remembered in whaling annals—November 20, 1820—dawned brilliant and relatively calm. By eight o'clock that morning a number of spouts were noticed on the lee bow. Watching them, the Nantucket whalers saw that there was a school of large whales engaged in blowing and playing on the surface of the sea.

Captain Pollard planned to take the school "head and head," as the saying went. The wheel of the *Essex* was "put up," all hands were called and the command to get the boats ready echoed down from the masthead. Springing to their line tubs, the crew bent on head irons and awaited the next order. Prospects looked better than ever. The reef of spouts was the longest of the voyage, and the giant mammals were enjoying to the utmost the squid they had found in great profusion.

Soon the *Essex* reached a position half a mile ahead of the school. Her main yards were backed so the vessel would remain as motionless as possible. The men were now ready to launch and meet the whales head-on.

"Hoist and swing," came the command, and eighteen out of the crew of twenty leaped into the three boats, leaving aboard only the steward and the cabin boy, Owen Coffin, who was Captain Pollard's nephew. The three boats were in the charge of Captain George Pollard, Mate Owen Chase and Second Mate Matthew Joy, whose boat a few days before had been stove in by an indignant whale. Soon the three craft were headed toward the school, and a short time later each had isolated a separate prey.

Running head-on toward the approaching whale, the whaleboat aimed to come in alongside the monster, heave the harpoon and sheer off fast enough to avoid the terrific death-dealing smash of the flukes.

Mate Chase soon struck his whale. Unfortunately he had chosen a stubborn fighter. The creature turned in its course instead of driving ahead at the feel of the iron. The monster stopped short, reversed course, and with its tail struck the whaleboat, breaking through the sides.

Chase cut the lines at once. The men stuffed their jackets into the openings and started rowing for the *Essex*, which they reached safely. Hoisting the boat aboard, the mate was about to start repairing her for a quick trip back to the line of spouts when he noticed a large sperm whale, probably eighty-five feet long, lying off the bow of the *Essex* with its great head facing the vessel.

Chase watched the giant, which spouted two or three times and then disappeared under the surface of the sea. A short time later it surfaced again and started swimming toward the *Essex.*

"His appearance and attitude gave us at first no alarm," Chase said later. "But while I stood watching his movements, and observing him but a ship's length off, coming down for us with great celerity, I involuntarily ordered the boy at the helm to put it hard up, intending to sheer off and avoid him. The words were scarcely out of my mouth before he came down upon us with full speed and struck the ship with his head, just forward of the forechains; he gave us such an appalling and tremendous jar as nearly threw us on our faces. The ship brought up as suddenly and violently as if she had struck a rock and trembled for a few minutes like a leaf. We looked at each other with perfect amazement, deprived almost of the power of speech."

Chase believed that the whale had been stunned by the tremendous concussion when it smashed through the bulkhead, and he was relieved when it started slowly swimming away. A long section of the false keel, loosened by the whale, came floating to the surface. The ship was leaking badly, and Chase soon rigged the pumps and set a signal for the other two boats to return.

Then it was that he saw the monster again. It was about "one hundred rods to leeward" and "apparently in convulsions." Leaping, twisting, thrashing, beating the water with its mighty flukes, crunching and snapping its enormous jaws as though "distracted with rage and fury," the monster terrified those who watched. Then it started swimming across "the bows of the ship to windward."

Owen Chase already had grave fears for the safety of the *Essex,* whether or not the whale attacked again. The vessel was beginning to settle down by the head despite the pumping. Chase decided to clear away the two remaining boats and to make plans for "getting all things ready to embark in them."

Suddenly one of the crew noticed that the giant cachalot was bearing down on the ship again. Petrified with fear, the sailors watched the huge mammal churning the ocean into foam as it tore through the water. Its head was unusually high above the surface, a one-hundred-ton battering ram.

Aiming straight for a point directly under the port cat head, the whale crashed completely through the bows as it hit, slid under the keel and went off to leeward. None of the men ever again saw the monster that delivered this death blow to the *Essex.*

The sailors were overwhelmed. That a whale would have the temerity to sink a whaleship was beyond their comprehension. Slowly they recovered. "The shock to our feelings was such I am sure none can have an adequate conception," said Chase later.

"We were dejected by a sudden, most mysterious, and over-whelming calamity," he went on. "We were more than a thousand miles from the nearest land, and with nothing but a light open boat, as the resource of safety for myself and companions. I ordered the men to cease pumping, ordering everyone to provide for himself. Seizing a hatchet at the same time, I cut away the lashings of the spare boat. . . ."

During the few minutes remaining before the ship rolled over, the men had time to save two navigation books, two quadrants, two trunks and two compasses. Barely ten minutes had elapsed since the first attack by the maddened whale. Pulling away from the plank-sheer, the crew watched with resignation as the vessel fell "over to windward and settled down in the water."

Meanwhile, some distance away, both Captain Pollard and the second mate were attempting to secure the whales they had already harpooned. One of the men in Second Mate Joy's boat, while busily engaged in passing short warp through a dead whale's fluke, happened to glance off toward where the *Essex* had last been seen, but there was no sign of her.

"Master Joy," he exclaimed, "where is the ship?" There was no answer the mate could give, and everyone in the boat became intensely worried. They cut the lines holding them to the whale and started rowing for the approximate location where they had left the *Essex.*

In the other boat, Captain Pollard had also noticed that his ship had disappeared. Bewildered, he ordered his whale cut free, and his boat started rapidly toward where the *Essex* had been.

"The Captain's boat was the first that reached us," Chase explained later. "He stopped about a boat's length off, but had no power to utter a single word.

"I could scarcely recognize his countenance, he appeared so

much altered, awed and overcome with the oppression of his feelings, and the dreadful reality that lay before him.

"He was in a short time, however, enabled to address the inquiry to me, 'My God, Mr. Chase, what is the matter?' I answered, 'We have been stove by a whale.' I then briefly told him the story. After a few minutes of reflection he observed that we must cut away her masts and endeavor to get something out of her to eat."

The three boats then pulled to where the ship lay floating on her beam ends. Using the boat hatchets, the men cut away the shroud lanyards and then were able to chop through the masts, after which the *Essex* righted.

Using a quadrant in Mate Chase's boat, Captain Pollard then observed a meridian altitude of the sun to get his latitude. He estimated that their position was then 0° 40' South and 119° West longitude. This would make the nearest land the Marquesas, 1500 miles to the southwest.

Meanwhile the crew started removing what stores they could. Taking off the booby hatch, they reached down into the after storeroom and discovered a 600-pound hogshead of dry biscuits. They also pulled out 200 gallons of water, which they divided among the three boats. Two turtles, firearms, bullets, powder, percussion caps, files, rasps and boat nails completed the complement of each whaleboat.

That afternoon the wind began to blow and a towline was made fast to the *Essex,* with one boat moored fifty fathoms away, a second eight fathoms beyond, the third eight more fathoms behind the second.

At dawn the wind was still blowing and the sea was rough. When the sun came up the whalers went aboard the water-logged *Essex* and took light spars to use in the small boats for masts and canvas for sails. All three craft were fitted with two masts and a flying jib. Two spritsails were finished, each with double bands. The topside of each boat was raised about half a foot, which gave them additional free board for the expected storms.

For two days and two nights the three boats with the twenty men aboard lay alongside the wreck, hoping another whaler might appear. None came, for in 1820 other vessels in the area were few and far between.

Finally Captain Pollard called a council of his mates to decide what should be done. By this time the deck on the *Essex* was starting to give way and the cargo of oil was beginning to break up, spreading over the sea. It was agreed by the whalers that they should start within a few hours, at noon on November 22, 1820, and sail south-southeast. They decided against heading northwest toward the Sandwich Islands, for they believed that they would encounter bad storms along that course.

Actually, while they had been debating, the *Essex* and the three whaleboats had drifted across the equator. When Captain Pollard took his final sight before starting out, they were in longitude 120° West and latitude 0° 13′ North.

"Taking all things with consideration," wrote Chase, "it would be most advisable to shape our course by the wind to the southward, as far as 25° or 26° South latitude, fall in with the variable winds and then endeavor to get eastward to the coast of Chili or Peru."

Chase's whaleboat had been damaged. It was planned that six men were to make the journey with him, leaving seven men each on the two remaining craft. The men agreed upon daily rations of one biscuit, which weighed nineteen ounces, and half a pint of water.

On November 27, five days later, Chase's boat was struck by an unidentified fish. To repair the boat, provisions had to be jettisoned. All this time schools of dolphins played around them but evaded attempts to catch them.

On the last day of November the crew of each boat killed a turtle and drank the blood. Then they turned the reptiles upside down, made a fire inside the shell and cooked and ate the meat.

On December 3, Second Mate Joy's boat disappeared during the night, but was sighted by the others the next morning. Five days later a gale smashed into the little fleet and the masts were unshipped. The storm was hard enough to endure during the day, but the night was dreadful. Heavy squalls battered the craft. Lightning flashed, illuminating the otherwise complete blackness that shrouded them. Fortunately the gale ended without causing serious damage.

Observations taken December 9 indicated that the boats were in 17° 40′ South latitude. Flying fish that smashed against the sails were quickly eaten, bones and all.

Of this period Owen Chase wrote: "The privation of water is justly ranked among the most dreadful of the miseries of our life; the violence of raging thirst has no parallel in the catalogue of human calamities. It was our hard lot to have felt this in its extremest force, when necessity compelled us to seek resource from one of the offices of nature."

It was essential a few days later to cut the rations in half. The men were now so desperate that when barnacles were discovered on the bottom of the boats they scraped them off and ate them.

On December 20 land was sighted. Owen Chase called it "the blessed vision before us," and told of how the seamen "shook off the lethargy of our senses." It appeared at first a "low, white beach and lay like a basking paradise before our longing eyes."

Landing with difficulty on the rocky shore, the men searched for water, but it was several days before a spring was found, which could be used only at low water. A few fish were caught, some birds were trapped and eggs were devoured.

Owen Chase's observation indicated a latitude of 24° 40′

South, longitude 120° 40′ West. He decided that they had landed at Ducie's Island. Actually it was Henderson Island, 2000 miles northwest of Ducie's. Not far away, two to three days sail under fair conditions, lay Pitcairn's Island, a land of relative plenty where they would have been welcomed and fed by the mutineers from the *Bounty* and their families. But the twenty whalers knew nothing of this.

After the discovery of water three of the men expressed a desire to be left on the island. Because food was a vital problem, it was agreed that William Wright and Seth Weeks, both of Barnstable, and an Englishman, Thomas Chapple, would be allowed to remain. This arrangement lightened each boat by one man.

Before the main party sailed away, a gruesome discovery was made of eight human skeletons in a cave hidden by tangled underbrush. Side by side, it was evident that the victims, weakened by lack of food and water, had crawled there to die. Further search revealed the name *Elizabeth* carved into a tree near the site. Possibly a ship by that name had foundered nearby and the survivors had reached the island, only to perish later.

This encounter hurried the departure of the seventeen whalers. First, however, Captain Pollard wrote an account of the *Essex* disaster, enclosed it in a tin box and nailed it to a tree.

On December 27, 1820, the three men who had chosen to stay waved farewell to the others as they pulled off the rocky shore. Captain Pollard now believed that he could reach Easter Island, to the northeast. But contrary winds and currents made him abandon this objective, and he was forced to choose a new goal: Juan Fernández Island, 2000 miles away, off the South American coast.

On January 10, 1820, Second Mate Matthew Joy died. He was sewn into his blanket with a stone tied to his feet. Then the body was consigned to the deep with prayers.

A severe gale began on January 12, and that night Chase's whaleboat lost sight of the other two. The mate marked down the position at the point of separation as latitude 32° 16' South and longitude 112° 20' West. He wrote: "For many days after this accident, our progress was attended with dull and melancholy reflections. We had lost the cheering of each other's faces."

Alone now, he had to make further cuts in the bread allowance. One and a half ounces a day was the new apportionment, and shortly afterward one of the five men, Richard Peterson, was caught stealing bread. Chase made him return it, and the unfortunate thief was so penitent that he then refused to eat his tiny ration, thus slowly starving himself.

A large shark began to follow the boat but did no serious damage. Porpoises were sighted on January 16, and two days later many whales were seen spouting. Peterson, refusing food to the end, died of starvation on January 20, and his remains were given a sea burial in latitude 35° 07' South, longitude 105° 46' West.

The other sailors were in terrible condition by now. One day the mate tore the leather from the steering oar and began to chew it. Not a man was strong enough to steer, and the boat drifted along by itself during this period.

A terrible day was endured February 8, 1821. Their sufferings were then drawing to a close, and death faced every man. Isaac Cole had become delirious, and about nine o'clock in the morning developed "a most miserable spectacle of madness." All that day he lay in the greatest pain and misery, "groaning piteously until four o'clock, when he died in the most horrible and frightful convulsions."

Preparations for burial were made, but Chase decided to bring up the painful but necessary subject of keeping Cole's body for food. "Our provisions could not last beyond three days," Owen later wrote. "I have no language to paint the anguish of our souls in this frightful dilemma." After a discussion the group agreed that to keep alive they would use the corpse for sustenance.

The food lasted until the morning of February 15. During the interval their strength returned. The very next day a cloud was sighted, which the mate believed was hanging over the island of Más Afuera. Early the next day the boy Thomas Nicholson resigned himself to death and lay down in the boat.

At seven the same morning the man at the steering oar, Ben Lawrence, suddenly shouted, "There's a sail!"

"The earliest of my recollections are that immediately I stood up," Chase explained later, "gazing in a state of abstraction and ecstasy upon the blessed vision of a vessel about seven miles off.

"The boy, too, took a sudden and animated start from his despondency and stood up to witness the probable instrument of his salvation. Our only fear was now that she would not discover us, or that we might not be able to intercept her course, we having put our boat immediately as well as we were able in a direction to cut her off, and found to our great joy that we sailed faster than she did."

Approaching closer to the craft, which now they recognized as a brig, the three survivors were gratified to notice that the vessel was shortening sail, thus allowing them to come alongside. She was the *Indian* of London, and her master was Captain William Crozier.

"I made an effort to assist myself along the side but my strength failed me altogether," Chase later stated. "We must have formed at that moment, in the eyes of the Captain and his crew, a most deplorable and affecting picture. . . .

"Our cadaverous countenances, sunken eyes, and bones just starting through the skin, with the ragged remnants of clothes stuck about our sunburned bodies, must have produced an appearance to him affecting and revolting to the highest degree."

The first food allowed the three survivors was a gruel made from tapioca, given them in tiny doses at first, after which the portions were increased. In a few days the three were able to walk.

They had been picked up in latitude 33° 45′ South, longitude 81° 03′ West. At noon that February 18 when they were rescued, the *Indian* actually sighted Más Afuera, proving Chase right in estimating his position. It was figured that the twenty-seven-foot whaleboat had been at sea for nearly three months. They had drifted, sailed and rowed 3700 miles!

On February 25 the *Indian* sailed into Valparaiso, Chile, where the three whalers were landed.

During this period the boats of Captain Pollard and Second Mate Joy were suffering comparable hardships. When he could no longer see Chase's whaleboat, Captain Pollard thought that his mate's craft had been sunk. Third Mate Obed Hendricks had been transferred to take command of the other boat after Joy's death.

These two craft attempted a course that would allow them to reach the island of Juan Fernández, 2000 miles distant. However, on January 27 heavy seas came sweeping in and the two whaleboats were separated. They were then in latitude 35° South and longitude 100° West. The craft in the charge of Third Mate Obed Hendricks was never seen or heard from again.

Finally, on February 23, 1821, the island of Santa Maria off Chile was sighted. By this time only two men in Captain Pollard's boat were still alive, Pollard himself and Charles Ramsdell. That same day the two survivors were seen by the Nantucket whaleship *Dauphin,* whose master was Captain Zimri Coffin. The men were taken aboard and given the best of care. They finally reached Valparaiso, where they were soon reunited with the three other shipmates who had arrived previously.

Captain Pollard could not forget the trio they had left behind at Henderson Island. Commodore Ridgely, commander of the *Constellation,* was then ashore in Valparaiso. He arranged for Captain Raine of the British ship *Surrey,* on his way to Australia, to stop at Henderson Island and rescue the three men, if they were still alive.

Back at Henderson Island the whalers had been successful in their efforts to get enough food. On April 5, 1821, they were aroused by the sound of a cannon. Rushing to the highest point of land, they saw a welcome sight: the *Surrey* standing in toward the island. The castaways, who had been marooned on Henderson Island for 102 days, were soon taken aboard the British vessel, which headed at once for civilization.

After landing in Australia, they sailed to London, where Britisher Thomas Chapple went to his home and Weeks and Wright took a ship for Boston.

Meanwhile, Captain Pollard, exhausted by worry and responsibility, had a relapse in Valparaiso and was sick in bed for a considerable length of time. Eventually he took passage for home on the *Two Brothers.*

Owen Chase, Ramsdell, Lawrence and Nicholson arrived home on the Nantucket whaler *Eagle* on August 9, 1821. Word of the tragedy had preceded them, and the wharves were packed with Nantucketers as the four survivors slowly made their way from the ship toward their homes.

Captain Raine had taken the tin box with Captain Pollard's letter from Henderson Island. Its contents have been preserved:

Account of the loss of the SHIP *Essex* of Nantucket, in North America, (written at Ducie's Island Dec. 20) 1820, commanded by George Pollard, junior, which shipwreck happened on the 20th day of November 1820, on the equator in long. 119° W., done by a large whale striking her in the bow, which caused her to fill with water in about ten minutes. We got what provision and water the boats could carry and left her on the 22'd of November and arrived here this day with all hands except one black man who left the ship at Ticamus. We intend to leave tomorrow, which will be the 26th of December, 1820, for the continent. I shall leave with this a letter for my wife, and whoever finds and have the goodness to forward it, will oblige an unfortunate man, and receive his sincere wishes.

George Pollard, Junior

Captain Pollard was the last of the survivors to reach Nantucket, due to the relapse he had suffered in Valparaiso. Eventually he took passage on the *Two Brothers*. After resting briefly at home, he commanded the *Two Brothers* when she sailed again on November 12, 1821. But his hard luck stayed with him.

Almost half a year later, the *Two Brothers* was wrecked on a reef north of the Sandwich Islands, and again Captain Pollard faced an open-boat journey. A few days later he and his men were all rescued by the whaler *Martha*.

Believing himself "utterly ruined," Pollard decided to give up the sea. "No owner will ever trust me with a whaler again, for all will say I am an *unlucky* man."

Arriving home April 27, 1825, the captain never went to sea again, and later became a town watchman.

~~~~~~~~~~~

CHAPTER 6

The Halifax Disaster

On the morning of December 6, 1917, the *Mount Blanc* and the *Imo* collided in Halifax harbor, causing what forever afterward has been called the Halifax Disaster.

In New York the French ammunition craft *Mount Blanc* had put aboard a deadly cargo of picric acid, benzol and trinitrotoluene, and was on her way inbound to Bedford Basin for convoy. The Norwegian ship *Imo,* loaded with goods for Belgian relief, as a huge sign in red letters on a white background stated, was outbound.

For some strange reason, forever to be unknown, the two craft came together, with the *Imo* knifing deep into the vitals of the ammunition ship, spilling the benzol against the rest of the cargo. The benzol poured into the picric acid, setting it afire, and soon the great *Mount Blanc* was ablaze.

Ordering full-speed astern, the captain of the *Imo* slowly backed her toward the Dartmouth shore. Aboard the *Mount Blanc* the forty-two members of the ship's company launched two lifeboats, rowed desperately for the opposite shore, landed on the beach and disappeared almost at once into the dense woods there. They knew what lay ahead!

Alone, but noticed by hundreds along the shore, the blazing *Mount Blanc* drifted down the harbor toward the open sea. All over the city the day was barely beginning for the people of

Halifax. Workmen were engaged at their duties in the various factories along the waterfront, while businessmen were journeying to their offices. Housewives had just sent their children off to school and were getting ready to do their shopping.

Then, cutting through the early morning noises, came the sound of the fire alarm, for a watcher had sighted the burning ship and notified the fire department. Many workers looked out into the harbor at the *Mount Blanc.* Frightened but fascinated, they watched the beautiful blue-green flames leaping higher and higher into the air, changing to great billows of grayish smoke far overhead.

Suddenly, as they watched spellbound, there was a terrific, cataclysmic concussion, followed a split-second later by a detonation that overwhelmed everything. The *Mount Blanc* had exploded.

A tidal wave roared toward shore, swept over the entire waterfront, then receded almost as fast as it had formed. Tugs, schooners and ships all thumped on the harbor bottom as the wave rushed back into the bay. The *Imo,* battered ashore by the wave, was pushed high on the beach at Dartmouth. The explosion literally wiped out every home, office building, church, school and factory along the waterfront, leaving only rubble and rubbish in their places.

Stewart Webb, a survivor of the holocaust, was a twenty-five-year-old hatch boss in charge of loading 96-pound bags of flour into the hold of the *Curaca,* a vessel tied up to a dock in Halifax. In 1978 when he talked with me, he remembered very well his experiences during and after the explosion. All around him people had died, but he emerged alive. He told of believing that his craft had sunk when the wave caused by the explosion struck. After regaining his feet, he looked out but could see nothing as the heavy black smoke surrounded him. Something hit him on the head so that he again fell to the deck. Stunned, he took a few minutes to realize that he would have to move. A cable swinging above him caught his eye. Grasping it, he swung out over the side of the ship, landing in the stays of the main rigging.

"I caught hold of the rigging and started climbing." From about twenty feet above the deck he could see that the sun was shining. He looked around. "Everything was burning. Everything was on fire." Entire blocks of buildings were rubble. The *Curaca,* now away from the pier, was still rolling.

As Stewart returned to the deck of the ship, he realized there was no one visible. Then a man appeared on the wharf and took a line Webb threw him from the stern and another from the bow to make the ship fast. Gradually he found two men on the vessel able to move, Jim Shields and a man named Larry, both blackened and practically unrecognizable. The three of them hunted throughout the *Curaca,* finding six men injured but still breathing, as well as other bodies. They transferred the living to a tugboat passing late that afternoon, and all nine men went to Campbell's Wharf.

Stewart Webb did not see anything left of the *Mount Blanc,* but other sources say that a battered hulk, the remains of the ammunition ship, could be seen protruding from the harbor water. The Halifax Narrows will always be associated with this terrible explosion. From 1600 to 2000 people were killed there, and 6000 others were injured. Ten thousand persons were made homeless, and total damage amounted to more than $35 million.

CHAPTER 7

The Wreck of the
Jennie M. Carter

One of the best-remembered New England wrecks, at least by past generations, was that of the three-masted schooner *Jennie M. Carter,* perhaps because no one ever came away from her alive. The *Carter* had a gross tonnage of 296.22, her length was 130 feet, her breadth 35 feet and her depth 10 feet. She was built at Newton, Maryland, in 1874, and her home port was Providence, Rhode Island. The details of just what happened will always be in doubt, but a fairly reliable series of events can be deduced.

At five o'clock on the morning of Friday, April 13, 1894, the schooner was seen drifting along Salisbury Beach opposite the end of the plank road by a Mr. Fowler, a resident of Hampton, Massachusetts. Evidently even then there was not a soul aboard. An hour later the lifesavers at Plum Island Point sighted her just as she went aground. The crew at the station were at that moment sitting down to breakfast. They all sprang up, donned oilskins and rubber boots, and launched their lifeboat. Crossing the harbor, the surfboat proceeded up Black Rocks Creek to the scene of the wreck.

Meanwhile, Fowler and a companion had followed the *Carter* along the beach. When she grounded they waited a short time, then climbed up into her chains and reached her deck. To their surprise they did not find a single person aboard.

About an hour later the lifesavers boarded the wreck, and Surfman Phillip H. Creasey discovered that a clock in the cabin was still going. When he tossed it ashore the hands registered 10:25.* Also taken ashore were the compass, the ship's papers and the quadrant. By this time the schooner's back was broken by her heavy cargo of paving blocks, and there was no hope of salvaging her.

According to reports the *Carter* was carried directly over the Breaking Rocks Ledge where the *Sir Francis* had hit in 1873, then drifted ashore opposite the present site of the old Ocean Echo, a dancehall of the period.

On April 10 at ten o'clock in the morning the *Carter* had been sighted by the schooner *Smuggler* off Highland Light, her rudder missing and the jibboom, bowsprit and foretopmast gone as well. The *Smuggler* lay by for two hours, but at that time Captain Wesley T. Ober of the *Carter* was confident that he could reach land without assistance, and so the *Smuggler* sailed away.

Later the new yawl of the *Carter* was discovered near Sandy Beach by Patrolman C. M. Noyes of the Plum Island Station. The handle of a gripsack was found tied to the gunwhale of the boat, indicating that perhaps someone had put his belongings in the yawl as an effort was made to reach shore. Keeper Elliot of the Plum Island Lifesaving Station did not concur in this theory, believing instead that all the crew were gathered at the anchor attempting to lower away when a great wave came over the side and took every man into eternity.

For some time on the morning of the disaster there was a

---

*The clock is now in the home of a resident of Quincy, Massachusetts. He obtained it from Herbert E. Hanson of Dorchester, who in turn received it from a relative who had been given it by Surfman Creasey a few years after the disaster. According to the present owner, the clock still runs, although it is so noisy that he winds it up only for visitors.

report that every man in the crew had reached shore safely and had been taken up to the Hampton Beach Hotel. But a visit by interested people disclosed that no one from the wreck had been seen in Hampton, or anywhere else for that matter.

Another point of dispute was the alleged presence of a woman on board. When the lifesavers reached the wreck they discovered several lady's garments in the cabin. Later Captain A. L. Crowley of East Boston, brother of the *Carter*'s steward, stated that the captain's niece had made the trip. Later it was discovered that this was not true. Quite often the captain's wife went with him on sea journeys from port to port, but apparently she did not go on this trip. It is now believed that there were no women on board during the fatal voyage. There had been seven men on the schooner: the captain, the mate, the cook and four seamen, not one of whom was ever seen again alive.

By Friday afternoon the seas were washing off the deckhouses. The mizzenmast fell, and the other masts also went during that night. A large crowd, many of them disorderly, gathered on the beach to watch the craft break up.

The first body to come ashore was that of Sven Sigfred Petersson of Sweden, a twenty-five-year-old seaman who had been in America only a few years. The captain's body washed ashore near Knobb's Station, Plum Island, on April 19; his remains were sent to Sedgwick, Maine, there to be interred with those of his father.

A coat belonging to the mate, J. W. Preble, came ashore on April 23. A letter in it from West Harrington, Maine, was dated December 18, 1893.

The great cargo of paving stones was sold at auction on the morning of April 23. Crowds continued to go down to Salisbury Beach to view the remains of the wreck, which at least until 1956 showed a few blackened fragments of her keel at unusually low tides during times of a full or a new moon. The loss of the *Carter* was one of the most tragic shipwrecks of the area.

I still have one of the cobblestones that formed part of the cargo of the *Jennie M. Carter,* whose wooden ribs stuck up out of the sand the last time I visited her.

PART SEVEN

Supernatural Tales

CHAPTER 1

The Phantom Bark *Isidore*

More than a century ago the story of the bark *Isidore* was told and retold at hundreds of firesides all over Maine. Those who were superstitious said that there were many warnings that should have been heeded before the vessel sailed. Others claim that fate took a hand and that all aboard were predestined to perish. In any event, it was a weird departure the *Isidore* made from the harbor of Kennebunkport that November morning more than one hundred years ago. In place of the usual cheers and final shouts of encouragement, there seemed to be a vague premonition of approaching danger hanging over the wharf. Several of the women became so overwrought that they sobbed aloud.

On November 30, 1842, the bark dropped down the harbor and stood to the eastward on the starboard tack. Early that afternoon snow began to fall, and the wind freshened considerably. The *Isidore* made one or two tacks to work her way out of the bay. When the weather shut in about four o'clock, she was lost to the sight of the watchers ashore. In the morning the snow lay in drifts around town. Soon news came up from Ogunquit that the wreck of a large vessel was strewn along the shore. The *Isidore* had lost her battle with the elements, having hit the Bald Head Cliffs just north of Cape Neddick Nubble.

Then the stories of the strange warnings were remembered.

Two nights before the ship was scheduled to sail, a seaman named Thomas King, who had already received a month's pay in advance, had a terrible dream. In his nightmare the *Isidore* was wrecked and all aboard were lost. The dream so affected him that he visited Captain Leander Foss of the *Isidore* and begged to be excused from his contract, but the captain laughed at his uneasiness and told him to be on hand before sailing time. However, King hid in the woods until he could see the masts of the *Isidore* as the bark sailed out of the harbor. Later criticized when he reappeared, he was held in great respect when news of the foundering reached Kennebunkport.

The night before the departure of the bark another seaman had dreamed of seven coffins on the shores of the ocean. One was his own, according to a voice in the dream. He told his friends about it the next morning before the ship sailed. The seaman's body was one of those later recovered from the wreck.

A gravestone was erected in the cemetery at Kennebunkport to Captain Leander Foss of the *Isidore,* whose body was never found.

The *Isidore* has become the phantom ship of the Maine Coast. One day at dusk an Isles of Shoals fisherman saw a bark close-reefed, with shadowy men in dripping clothes who stared straight ahead from their stations on the bark. He and many others say the bark is still sailing the seas with its phantom crew.

～～～～

CHAPTER 2

Telepathy from the *Minerva*

Captain James Scott, an English mariner, married Mary Richardson on July 14, 1760. Because Captain Scott was at sea a good part of the time, Mary went to live in Marshfield with her brother Jeffrey Richardson II and his wife.

On March 4, 1787, Mary's brother was suddenly awakened about three o'clock in the morning. "Brother Scott has arrived and called to me," he told his wife.

"Go back to sleep," she admonished, "for it is only a dream."

Jeffrey Richardson was strangely troubled, however. "It was more than a dream," he replied, but tried to go back to sleep.

A short time later he heard his brother-in-law call to him again. The terror in his voice prompted Jeffrey to get up. Looking at the clock, he found it was about half-past three. Dressing hurriedly, he went to the door, opened it and was met by a swirling blizzard.

From the appearance of the high drifts around the house it evidently had been snowing for some time, and he noted from the northeasterly direction of the wind that it would be a fearsome night for sailors on the ocean, especially if they were off a lee beach.

Jeffrey went back to his bedroom, very disturbed, and again awakened his wife. "I am sorry, my dear, but I simply cannot get James from my mind. There is a great snowstorm outside from the northeast, and I am afraid that he is in serious trouble."

"What do you think you should do?" asked his wife. "It will not do any good to awaken Mary and get her to worry about it, will it?"

"No, perhaps not, but I am going to go down on the shore as soon as it gets lighter."

Jeffrey lay down without taking off his clothes and fell into a fitful sleep. About six o'clock that March morning such a mighty blast shook his home that he leaped to his feet. Glancing outside, he noticed that it was still snowing, but by now the first gray streaks of dawn were lighting up the sky despite the severe storm.

Jeffrey ate a quick breakfast, said good-bye to his wife, put on every storm-breaking garment he possessed, and left the house. It was a long walk to the Marshfield shore, but by seven o'clock he reached his destination.

A terrifying sight met his gaze. In every direction great masses of wreckage were strewn along the beach. Dead bodies were coming ashore, mixed in with seaweed and fragments of timbers. Other people were already exploring the beach, and Jeffrey approached one of them.

"Not a soul escaped alive," the man told Jeffrey. "And I don't think anyone was on the beach when the ship hit!"

"What was her name?"

"I don't know, but the lighter stuff floated ashore down near Cut River, and the quarterboard might be there. It is a terrible thing, isn't it? Not a single survivor!"

Jeffrey walked down the shore, stumbling through the wreckage and the snowdrifts, until he came upon an area where the timbers and cargo were piled three feet high. Several men were busily salvaging equipment from the surf and stowing it above the reach of the tide. Walking up to one of them, Jeffrey asked about the name of the vessel. One of the workers pointed to the south. "We did come across fragments of the quarterboard," he explained, "but you'll have to piece them together."

Jeffrey went in search of these bits of wreckage, and soon he came across what had once been the last two letters of a word, ending in *V A*. Continuing his hunt, he found a section bearing the letters *I N E* and *R*. The evidence was incontrovertible. Captain Scott's craft was named the *Minerva*.

Sick at heart, Jeffrey walked up and down the shore for the remainder of the morning. His wife and Mary Scott arrived at the scene shortly before noon, and he could postpone no longer telling them the terrible news that Captain Scott had been drowned almost within sight of his own home.

All three were spared the shock of watching the men working on the shore rescue the body of Mary's husband from the waves at low tide, for they had left the beach by then. Just before dark the remains of the master of the *Minerva* were carried to the church, and the family was notified shortly afterward.

Captain Scott's body was so marked by the surf that it was difficult to recognize him, but a large watch that he always carried with him confirmed the identification. This watch was kept by his widow for the remainder of her life. She moved to Essex Street in Boston shortly after the tragedy and is believed to have died there about 1820.

Her children grew and prospered, and one of them inherited the watch. In 1957 the watch was in the possession of Roscoe E. Scott, a resident of Cleveland, Ohio, from whom I was able to receive many particulars about this strange story of mental telepathy and death.

CHAPTER 3

~~~~~~~

Forget-me-not

About the year 1815 the rocky shores of Nahant attracted many Boston families during the summer months. Swallow Cave, John's Folly, Dorothy's Cove, Pulpit Rock and many other interesting locations became as familiar to Boston families as the Old State House and the Great Elm on Boston Common. Many prominent Bostonians, including social, political and literary figures, came to stay for a time at Little Nahant or Nahant.

Shortly after 1815 a Medford family journeyed to Nahant for the summer. The cottage into which they moved was next door to a summer home occupied by a group of Italians of high birth. One of them was a young man by the name of Faustino, who soon became interested in the young lady of the Medford family named Alice. Before long they were often seen together exploring the cliffs and crags of the rocky Nahant shore. When the first suggestions of fall began to show, the couple declared their engagement. In those days, however, it was customary to obtain parental consent of both families. Faustino's parents were still in Leghorn, Italy, also known as Livorno. Going to Boston, he made final arrangements to sail across the seas for this blessing on his coming wedding.

The last afternoon before the sailing the two lovers were sitting high on the Nahant ledges overlooking Egg Rock. As they sat gazing out over the spacious Atlantic, the thought came into the boy's mind of the legend of the forget-me-not flowers that grew at distant Egg Rock, and of the significance of these tiny blossoms. The story was that a girl who received from the hand of her lover a forget-me-not flower growing on that particular island should remain forever constant.

"Dear Alice," he cried, "give me this final opportunity to show my love. On yonder rock grows the forget-me-not flower. Let me journey out to it and secure for you the blossom taken from its highest pinnacle."

Alice tried to prevent him from making the trip to the rock, but he at once was afraid she doubted his courage. As he stood up, the faintest caress of a breeze caused his hair to blow across his brow, and Alice was seized with a premonition of danger. Again she implored him not to make the journey, but he ran down to Little Nahant Beach where his sailboat was moored.

An old man cautioned him, "Do not go out in your sailboat now, son, for the wind is rising. Wait for the next tide."

"The next tide will take me away from my beloved Alice," said the boy. "So it is now or never."

Waving a fond farewell to the watching Alice, he sailed for distant Egg Rock. But the winds were increasing rapidly, and the waves mounted higher and higher. White water showed all around Egg Rock when the sailboat approached, but the boy jumped lightly out and made the painter fast. Climbing up the sides of the high rock, he reached the sheltered nook where grew the forget-me-nots. High in the air he held them while he waved at his sweetheart a mile away in Nahant. Then he ran down to the sailboat.

By this time the surf and wind had combined to create a terrifying situation. Waves were breaking eight and ten feet high. When he finally pushed off with his sails set for shore, the wind took him far off course. The sailboat was soon in the breakers off the rocks where the couple had sat less than two hours before. Closer and closer the craft came. Alice, high on the cliff, watched with curious fascination this last act of her lover. Then came a mighty wave, larger than the others, which caught the sailboat in its merciless grasp and rushed the helpless lad with the speed of the wind toward the rocky cliffs. The poor boy looked up for a final moment into the eyes of his intended bride. Then the sailboat struck the rocks, broke up and was gone, together with Alice's lover. He had perished beneath the waves in a vain attempt to bring her the *Floure de Souvenance*.

Alice was brought back to her home in a state of collapse. Early the next morning fishermen knocked at her door; the body had been found and was, even then, lying on the great beach between Lynn and Nahant, covered with a blanket. Alice threw a shawl over her shoulders and rushed out of the house. A short time later she reached the beach. As she drew near, her sorrowing friends gathered around the lifeless body. She stood over her dead lover as they slowly withdrew the blanket from his form. His right hand was firmly clenched, and as she leaned over him, she noticed something still clutched in his grasp—a few stems of the flower for which he had given his life.

Taking one of the flower stems, Alice slowly walked away. Despite the terrible shock she was able to reach her home, but there she became desperately ill. Removed to her Medford residence, she never walked again. As the first flowers of spring made their appearance, Alice, mourning her lover to the end, died. She was buried in the family lot at Medford, and was soon forgotten by most of her friends.

But there were those who said that strange moanings— "Faustino! Faustino!"—were always heard near her grave whenever the wind began to rise, as though she were still protesting her lover's departure in that gathering October gale a century and a half ago.

Index